Daisy, Dad and the Huge, Small Suprise

Surprise and shock and nerves have different effects on everybody. Right then, I wanted to do what Dad and Linn and Rowan and Tor and Sandie and Rolf and Winslet were doing and whoop and hug and bark at Grandma and Stanley, but all I could think of was that I had to go for a wee *immediately*. ("Nervous bladder", Grandma informed me later.)

Once I'd got that sorted out (the weeing immediately bit), I found myself staring in the bathroom mirror as I wiped my hands with a cerise towel, listening to the laughing and whooping and barking going on downstairs, and tried to fathom why I suddenly felt so super-sad, at the same time as being super-happy.

Of course, I realized, as an invisible light bulb flickered on above my head. *Someone's missing...*

In two seconds I'd be downstairs, joining in the laughing etc., but a Very Important Person was missing from the family celebrations.

Mum – where are you...?

To find out more about Karen McCombie,
visit her website www.karenmccombie.com

ALLY'S WORLD

KAREN McCOMBIE

DAISY, DAD AND the HUGE, SMALL SURPRISE

SCHOLASTIC

ne books

ʊм'.)

First published in the UK in 2003 by Scholastic Children's Books
An imprint of Scholastic Ltd
Euston House, 24 Eversholt Street
London, NW1 1DB, UK
Registered office: Westfield Road, Southam, Warwickshire, CV47 0RA
SCHOLASTIC and associated logos are trademarks and or registered
trademarks of Scholastic Inc.

This edition published by Scholastic Ltd, 2007

Text copyright © Karen McCombie, 2003
The right of Karen McCombie to be identified as the author of this work
has been asserted by her.

Cover illustration copyright © Spike Gerrell, 2003

10 digit ISBN 0 439 95182 8
13 digit ISBN 978 0439 95182 1

British Library Cataloguing-in-Publication Data.
A CIP catalogue record for this book is available from the British Library

Printed in the UK by CPI Bookmarque, Croydon, CR0 4TD
Papers used by Scholastic Children's Books are made from wood grown in
sustainable forests.

3 5 7 9 10 8 6 4 2

This is a work of fiction. Names, characters, places, incidents and dialogues
are products of the author's imagination or are used fictitiously.
Any resemblance to actual people, living or dead, events or locales is
entirely coincidental.

www.scholastic.co.uk/zone

Contents

PROLOGUE

Dear Mum,
Wow.

Surprises sure can be, um, surprising. (Hey, Ally; what a stunning use of vocabulary. Not.)

It's just that one minute, there you are, ambling along, minding your own business, then; *whoosh!* a huge surprise comes up out of nowhere and slaps you in the face like a big, wet fish. (Ahem, how about *that* for more imaginative use of vocabulary? Better, huh? The World: "No.")

And you know I'm not talking about the sort of small surprises that pop up every day, like Rowan's latest hairdo (hairdon't), or Linn smiling (eek!), or Tor coming out with two sentences in a row (hallelujah, it's a miracle!). I'm not even talking about quite surprising surprises like finding Rolf burying the TV remote control in the flower bed, or coming across Winslet chewing her way through an entire pack of toilet rolls (de-*lish*!), or finding a gerbil snoozing in your sock drawer*.

Nope; *I'm* talking about full-blown, mega-tonne, jaw-dropping, *spine*-melting surprises. And my head is still reeling from the fact that there were four (*four!*) of them in a row recently. It started with Grandma's out-of-the-blue announcement, and then of course there was the whole thing with Daisy Woods, and *then*...

But what am I waffling about all this here for? After all, to get the whole amazing, unedited, un-expurgated story (I'm *really* showing off on the vocabulary front now), all you've got to do is turn the page.

In the meantime, I'd better go and help Tor with Snail Patrol (more of that later too). But I'll tell you one thing for nothing – there's no way you'd find *me* stroking slugs, like one small person I know**...

Love you lots,

Ally

(your Love Child No. 3)

* Tor said it had had a fight with another gerbil in its cage and needed a restful place to chill out. Glad to know my socks are so, er, calming. Maybe I should go over and sell them to that New Age-y shop just off the Broadway. The latest new hippy, healing therapy: "Stressed out? You need Love Socks..." Er, then again, maybe not.

** And it's not who you think I mean! (The mystery deepens…)

Chapter 1

JUST ANOTHER NORMAL(ISH) SATURDAY...

"Omigod! Ally! *Helppppppp!*"

For the last ten minutes I'd been sitting on one of the saggy, gently collapsing deckchairs in our garden, blowing bubblegum bubbles (then picking them off my nose when they burst) and pretending to read the new magazine I'd just bought when me and Tor were up at the Broadway this morning. But what I was *really* doing was staring over the top of my magazine in a super-spy style while I tried to figure out what exactly Tor was up to at the back of the garden, over by the shed. He seemed to be wafting his hands about, all animated, and ... and, well, having what looked like a really full-on conversation. Which was unusual on two counts:

1) He never talks enough to have what normal people would call a conversation; and

2) He was having this conversation with ... *himself.*

I was just mulling over the implications of this (should we get Michael our next-door-neighbour to check our little brother over? I mean, I know Michael's a vet and everything and not a doctor, but then Tor's brain is probably more like a *dolphin's* than a regular seven-year-old's brain), when Rowan made me jump by running out of the back door of the house, yelling like a banshee and holding her blood-red hands out in front of her.

Ah, yes ... it was just another regular Saturday in the Love family house, with my brother quietly losing his marbles and my sister appearing to have committed mass murder in the vicinity of the kitchen.

"What?" I blinked slowly up at Rowan, after pausing to suck in my most impressive bubble of bubblegum so far (i.e. it hadn't burst) and shielding the sun from my eyes.

Rowan looked like a maniac. And possibly an axe-wielding maniac from the look of her hands. Well, OK, not her hands exactly; the red-stained (orginally yellow) rubber gloves she was wearing. Of course, it wasn't just *that* that was making Rowan look like a maniac. The fact that she was wearing a black binliner and flip-flops didn't help her look too sane either. And Ro may be the reigning queen of bizarre hairdos, but today's was just *mental*.

"Oh, Ally! I've done something terrible!" she gasped and trembled, making her gravity-defying fringe wobble.

Too *right* she'd done something terrible – had she fixed her hair up like that for a bet? Or had she been playing Truth or Dare with her mates Chazza and Von and gone for the Dare option?

"What? Did you stick your fingers in an electrical socket or something?" I asked, eyeing her fringe warily. "Weren't you *listening* to that woman from the Royal Society for the Prevention of Accidents when she came to do that safety talk at school?"

Rowan frowned at me, my joke whizzing effortlessly over her head, then raised her eyes up in the general direction of her towering fringe.

"Oh, *that*! That was just something I was sort of trying out earlier. With this new hair wax stuff I got." She shrugged, making the plastic bag she was wearing rustle and sending drops of crimson red *whatever* dripping off her rubbery fingertips and on to the overgrown grass of our lawn.

You know, the ponytail on its own would have been OK, but why my airhead of a sister felt the need to wax her fringe till it stood straight up in spikes I have absolutely no idea. And neither did she, probably.

"So what *is* wrong? What's so terrible?" I tried to find out.

Had she given away her entire (weird) wardrobe to Oxfam in a moment of wild charitable-ness, and was now regretting it? At least *that* might explain why she was wearing a bin-bag... Or had she been whiling away a dull Saturday afternoon by recreating a scene from *The Texas Chainsaw Massacre* (her mate Chazza's favourite ever vintage horror movie) and accidentally killed some passing neighbours? Not *too* likely. (It sure would explain the red stuff on her hands, but our Rowan is a big wuss who can only watch horror movies from behind a metre-high barricade of sofa cushions.)

"You better come inside and see," said Ro mournfully, turning and rustling her way towards the back door, expecting me to follow her, I guess.

But getting *into* a saggy, gently collapsing deck-chair is one thing – getting *out* of it (in a hurry) is something else. Wriggling and panting like a geriatric frog, I finally escaped from the chair, still clutching my magazine (which I'd been holding upside down, I realized – wow, I'd make a truly, excellently *rotten* spy).

Before I followed her inside to see whatever it was that was flipping her out, I checked to see what Tor made of Rowan's fruitcake appearance, but clocked that he was oblivious, his back to us, with his hands covered in earth, happily joining Rolf in digging up the flowerbeds. At least that meant he'd given up that loopy talking-to-himself thing. (Not that having a frantic hole-digging race with your best dog buddy was entirely normal either.)

"So what's with the bin-bag frock?" I turned back to Rowan.

She was in the doorway by this time and whipped around to face me, putting one hand up on the white-painted doorframe, a look of pure alarm etched on her face.

"I'm dying..." she said bluntly.

It was only then that my heart skipped a beat – she'd dropped her gloved hand and left a vivid crimson print on the peeling white paint. Good grief – I'd been fooling about with her, but was Rowan *really* hurt? And really hurt that *bad*? Had she thrown the black bin-liner over herself to hide some huge, gaping wound, so that Tor wouldn't see her intestines dangling out or something?!?!

"In here..." she muttered, disappearing into the kitchen, which seemed ominously dark and gloomy after the dazzling sunshine outside.

"Ro?" I whispered nervously, scurrying in behind her and following her into the utility room, where All (eek!) Would Be Revealed...

"You … you see?" Rowan trembled, pointing at something. "It was an accident, Ally! Honest!"

She wasn't actually pointing in the direction of the cracked, old square sink in the corner, but that's where my eyes went first. I couldn't help it – the faded white of the porcelain was splattered in shades of wine and red, fading to lurid crimson. And the mound of soaking wet material piled up in the sink was palest of all – a vivid, shocking pink.

"I was being really careful! That's why I've got the gloves and bin-bag!" Ro squeaked at me, her eyes glued to a jumbled pile of fluffy white towels that Grandma had left sitting on top of the ironing board.

Ahhhhh…

My heart, which had leapt into my throat with fear and was quietly choking me, started sinking back down into my chest, where it was meant to be.

"Ro – when you said you were dying, you mean you were *dye*ing, right?" I checked with her.

"Of course!" nodded Rowan, pointing to a packet of Dylon Hand Dye in "Camellia", and not a severed limb, like I'd first thought she might. "I was just trying to tie-dye these baggy white cotton trousers that I got from the Cancer Research shop this morning!"

Rowan and her customizing projects ... she should stick to glueing mad stuff on to her T-shirts. At least the worst that happened with those was the time she ran out of fabric glue and used super-glue instead. She ended up spending the whole of the next week at school with her hands in her pockets, hiding the fact that she had silver and blue sequins stuck to every finger.

But what she'd done this time round ... let's just say Grandma wasn't going to see the funny side.

"How did it happen?" I asked, turning my attention to the white (ha!) towels.

"Well, I turned on the tap to wash the dye out and I guess I turned it on too hard, and all this water and dye splashed *everywhere*," Rowan shrugged helplessly. "Then I turned round and saw that I'd splattered the first towel, and I tried to pick it up and wash the dye out, only I got pink fingerprints and drips on the *next* towel, and so I tried to grab *that* and then... She's going to kill me, right?"

"Yeah, she's going to kill you," I nodded. All our brand new fluffy towels, which Grandma had only bought last week for us, looked like psychedelic Dalmatian towels – white with luminous pink spots. All over.

If *I* was Rowan I'd pack my bags and try and find a circus to run away and join *now*...

* * *

Plan A: that's what I'd called it. Not that there was a Plan B – Plan A (my brilliant Grandma-will-never-know scam to fix the towels) would work just fine. I was positive (*and* I had my fingers crossed).

"Ally! Look!" Tor gasped, pointing at the poster in the newsagent's near the toy shop.

We'd come up to Crouch End Broadway with Rowan, just to give her a bit of moral support, but hanging out in Woolworths with her while she tried to find a bottle of dye remover (Plan A) was way too dull, so me and Tor had left Rowan to it while we mooched around across the road in Wordplay, flicking through the book department and then trying on the false noses they had in the pocketmoney-toy section of the shop. We were still giggling when we stumbled out and saw the poster.

"'The Russian State Circus'," I read aloud, gazing up at the technicolour sign.

"They're coming to Alexandra Palace! This week!" Tor said excitedly, like I hadn't read the rest of the poster. "Miss Woods is going! She said so!"

"Who's Miss Woods?" I asked.

"Teacher!" Tor shrugged.

OK – he must mean the teacher person at the summer craft classes (or whatever they were called) that he was going to. She must be the person who was responsible for the giant papier mâché sculpture of a slug and the photo frame made out of Lucozade bottle tops that Tor had brought home recently.

"Oh, right," I replied, remembering Grandma's strained smile of pleasure when he'd presented her with his twig 'n' twine toothbrush holder as a gift last week.

"So, can we all go?" Tor asked hopefully.

"Yeah, but look how much it costs," I grimaced, checking out the prices. There was no way that Dad could take me and Tor and Linn and Rowan and still be able to pay the red phone bill that was sitting on top of the rickety writing desk in the living room.

I was just thinking that I'd talk to Dad about maybe taking Tor on his own (a zillion times cheaper) when a mental fringe with a girl attached to it rushed up to us. I'd sussed out by now that it didn't matter whether Rowan was deliriously happy or downright miserable, with that demented fringe she'd look permanently startled, whatever.

"Did you get the dye remover OK?" I asked her.

Rowan shook her head, which *should* have meant

bad news, but weirdly she was smiling. Uh-oh. What did that mean?

"But if Plan A failed..." I frowned at her.

"...there's Plan B!" she beamed, pulling something out of the Woolies plastic bag she was holding.

"Rowan," I began, staring at what she was holding, "you have gone completely mad."

Rowan grinned some more, like I'd given her the best compliment ever.

Oh, good grief. Should I order a straitjacket now? One with sequins sewn on it, of course...

Chapter 2

HUGE SURPRISE, NO. 1

"Ooh, vanilla, please!"

"OK," I nodded, closing the front door behind Sandie with one hand, and holding a tall glass of homemade milkshake in the other.

Sandie had just arrived for tea (and to stay the night), and the first thing I'd said after hello was did she fancy a milkshake too, and what flavour did she want. It would have been rude not to, considering her eyes had lit up and she'd more or less said hello to the milkshake instead of me. Not that we had any other tall glasses left, not after Rolf chased a cat that wasn't Colin on to the draining board the other day and sent five out of six newly washed tall glasses clattering on to the floor like breakable skittles. So Sandie'd just have to have her milkshake in a big mug. Or maybe a small vase.

"No! Make that chocolate," Sandie faffed.

"Whatever."

"Er, no – vanilla. Definitely."

"Vanilla, then."

"No – sorry, chocolate!"

"OK..."

"Um, then again ... strawberry!"

One thing you should never give Sandie Walker is a choice. She's a top best friend in many ways – loyal, kind, laughs at my jokes – but her dithering can send you demented. I should have just *told* her what flavour milkshake she was getting and left it at that.

"Strawberry ... fine," I nodded, as we padded along the hall. "And then we can go into the garden, 'cause tea won't be ready for ages yet."

"Yum!" Sandie grinned. "I'm starving! So who's cooking tonight?"

Her smile froze as soon as she followed me into the kitchen. Bad luck, Sandie. You've chosen to come the night that it's Rowan's turn to make the tea...

"Hi," Rowan waved absently in Sandie's direction, as her head bobbed behind a cookbook.

Sandie raised her eyebrows at me, while I grabbed a carton of milk out of the fridge. Maybe it was Rowan's standing-to-attention fringe that was amazing her, or maybe she was impressed with the fact that Rowan was flicking through a cookbook, since my sister never normally bothers with nonsense like recipes and measurements, preferring to make up her menus as she goes along (and trust me, it *shows*).

"What are you making?" Sandie asked Ro, leaning over the back of her chair and squinting at the pretty foody pictures.

(Lucky for me Sandie was doing that; it gave me a chance to swill the skinny glass vase from the windowsill under the tap. Didn't suppose strawberry 'n' dust 'n' dead fly flavour was all that mouthwatering.)

"This Tuna Pasta Melt, thing," said Rowan, pointing to one of the open pages.

"Mmm ... 'tuna, with tricolour pasta in tomato, garlic and basil sauce, sprinkled with mozzarella cheese'!" Sandie drooled as she read out the recipe description.

"Yeah, sounds nice, doesn't it?" Rowan turned and beamed at my appreciative best mate.

Ha, ha, ha – how trusting and gullible is Sandie? Even *I* knew that tonight's meal sounded too good to be true.

"But I'll have to adapt it a bit," Rowan continued, turning back to the list of ingredients. "We haven't got any tuna, so I'm going to open a couple of tins of sardines instead. And we're right out of pasta, but we've got tons of rice. And 'cause we haven't got any chopped tomatoes, or garlic, *or* basil, I thought I'd use a tin of tomato soup and chuck an Oxo cube in it to spice things up…"

Great. Instead of Tuna Pasta Melt, Rowan – our resident family poisoner – was going to give us Fishy Rice Gloop.

"But we've got cheese, right?" I asked hopefully. I mean, the only thing that was likely to make this Fishy Rice Gloop even *vaguely* edible was if it was swamped with grated cheddar or something. (I'd bet three trillion pounds that there wasn't going to be any mozzarella lurking in our fridge.)

"Yes, we've got some of those little Dairylea triangles," Rowan said chirpily.

Fantastic. Fishy Rice Gloop with triangles of soft cheese left over from Tor's packed lunches blobbed on top. Looked like I'd have to fake stomach ache again (and fast) to get out of eating Rowan's latest disaster.

Speaking of Rowan's disasters, her most recent one – this afternoon's – was just about to resurface.

"Er, girls…" Dad's voice suddenly boomed, as he squelched into the kitchen wearing nothing but a large pink towel tied around himself and leaving a trail of wet footprints behind him. "Oh, hello, Sandie! Didn't hear you come in!"

"Uhhh ... hello, Mr Love," Sandie mumbled, dropping her head so she didn't have to look at my skinny, tall dad in all his embarrassing half-nakedness.

Good grief; now Dad – fresh out of the shower after washing a day's worth of axle grease and bicycle oil off himself – and Sandie were *both* blushing; their cheeks the same shade of pink as the towel Dad was gripping tightly on to.

"What's up, Dad?" I asked, although I knew *exactly* what was up. And could feel my cheeks joining in the general pink glow that was radiating in our kitchen. Apart from the fact that Rowan had implicated me and Tor in the Great Towel Disaster (which Dad was just about to uncover), it was kind of icky that my father was showing himself up to be no six-pack, muscly, WWF type in front of other people. I mean, *we* all know he looks like a whippet with malnutrition with his shirt off, which is why my entire family has banned him from cutting the grass in summer wearing anything less than a T-shirt. (We're scared some-one'll call the RSPCP – the Royal Society for the Prevention of Cruelty to Parents – to report us Love kids for working him too hard and not feeding him enough pies or something.) But it's madly mortifying that anyone else should catch a glimpse of how weedy he is (bless him). I mean, couldn't he at least *try* to grow more than just *one* hair on his chest?

"It's just ... well, since when did we have pink towels?" Dad asked me and Ro, his dark eyebrows bobbing about quizzically on his forehead like two hairy caterpillars doing a barn dance.

"Since today!" Rowan answered brightly. "I dyed all those new towels Grandma bought for us!"

Yep, Dad was currently hiding his modesty behind Plan B. Faced with pink spots she couldn't get rid of, Rowan had bought herself another packet of Dylon Hand Dye – in "Camellia" – and spent the rest of the afternoon in a dyeing and drying frenzy.

"Um ... *why*?" Dad asked, distractedly scratching his dark, spiky hair with one hand, then dropping it down fast and regaining his vice-like grip on the towel, just in *case* it felt like sneakily dropping to his ankles once his guard was down.

"Because on all the home-decorating programmes on TV they're saying that pink is in, and white is absolutely out!" Rowan enthused.

"White's out?" Dad replied dubiously.

"Absolutely!" Rowan lied herself silly.

"But this funny shade of pink ... it doesn't really go with the bathroom, does it?"

Well, spotted, Dad. When me and Tor were hanging up the newly spun-dried pink monstrosities in the bathroom earlier, we were nearly blinded by the clash of cerise versus the pillar-box red of the walls.

"Pink and red! They're ... they're the hippest new combination!"

I nudged Sandie, handing her the small vase of strawberry milkshake I'd just mixed up for her, and nodded towards the back door. I could still hear Rowan prattling on, trying to convince Dad that our house was now at the cutting edge of interior design thanks to her dyeing efforts, when me and Sandie flopped down on to the grass outside, where an assortment of tiny, buzzy, flappy, flying things were still happily buzzing, flapping and flying around in the warm evening air.

"What's Tor doing?" asked Sandie, scrunching her eyes against the low sun and peering at my little brother, who appeared to be chattering away to himself while he played with his homemade *Star Wars* battleship (the top of the laundry basket covered in tin foil) while Rolf and Winslet snoozled in the shade close by him.

"I'm not sure, but whatever it is, he was doing it

earlier," I told Sandie, recalling this afternoon's spying mission with my upside-down magazine. "Hey, what's that?"

The "that" I was referring to was a very cute daisy chain strung around Sandie's neck.

"Oh, *this* thing!" Sandie giggled self-consciously, putting one trembly finger on the fresh flowers. "Billy made it for me, when we were up at Ally Pally earlier!"

Urgh ... I hadn't seen that one coming. My two best friends, i.e. my two best friends who – during my whole history of knowing them both – couldn't *stand* each other, had been going out for an entire week now, and I couldn't get my head around it, which is why I was trying really, *really* hard not to bring the subject up. I mean, how can that happen? Two people who have got precisely nothing (apart from me) in common; who whinged about each other constantly ("Why's Billy got to be so loud and show-offy?", "Why's Sandie so wet and wimpy?"), suddenly decide to be huge snogging buddies? It just didn't make sense...

Rowan tried to explain it to me (since Billy and Sandie sure couldn't, what with the radioactive glow of lovey-doveyness melting their brains). She said that it happens all the time, men and women falling in love, when ten minutes ago they hated each other so much they wouldn't have given the other one 20p for a Pay-On-Entry public loo, no matter *how* desperate for a widdle they were. In fact, Ro said it happens in movies all the time, like in *When Harry Met Sally* and … and loads of others, only I'd stopped listening by that time 'cause I was in a tizz. I mean, I pretty much hated Darth Maul from *The Phantom Menace* and I certainly didn't like shouty Mr Horace, our maths teacher. So, according to Rowan, did that mean I'd fall in love with a crap fictitious character with really bad make-up? Or – worse still – in ten years time or something, was I destined to end up married to the crabbiest, baldest teacher at Palace Gates School, with all the kids calling me Mrs Horse-Arse?! Argghhhhh…

But I'd done it now, I'd given Sandie an opportunity to tell me what a lovely guy Billy was, and what it felt like to kiss him (no! someone give me earplugs now before I retch!!). She was smiling coyly, her cheeks were flushed as pink as Dylon Hand Dye in "Camellia", and she was opening her mouth ready to tell me all the slushy, gushy details when…

"Ally! Tor!" Linn barked from the back door.

The Grouch Queen must have just got back home from her Saturday/holiday job at the trendy clothes shop up on the Broadway.

"What?" I spun my head around towards her, very glad (for once) to be interrupted by my inevitably bad-tempered big sis.

"Grandma's here. *And* Stanley. You've got to come in, *now*," Linn informed us, like the born-to-be sergeant major that she is.

Gee, what was the big deal? I loved Grandma (still do, natch), and I liked her boyfriend Stanley too (even though he had spectacularly hairy ears), but why did we have to zoom inside like it was some fancy occasion? Yeah, so Grandma only popped in at the weekends now and again (since she was with us every day of the week), but it still didn't exactly rate as spectacular as the Queen dropping by for a cup of tea and some Fishy Rice Gloop.

Still, I wasn't going to complain about the distraction – anything to get me away from Sandie's descriptions of how "cuddlyable" Billy was (blee...).

I bolted for the house, but still managed to get beaten to it. The order of arrival from the garden was: Rolf (hoping Linn's shout translated as "More food for dogs!"), Winslet (ditto), a cat that wasn't Colin (ditto, but for cats), Tor (who'd stopped speaking to himself long enough to race inside to see his beloved gran), Sandie (beating me because

I tripped over Spartacus the tortoise on the way), and bringing up the rear ... me.

"Hello, dears!" Grandma beamed girlishly, with Stanley beaming in tandem by her side, as our bundle of pets and people thundered in the back door.

Hmmm ... I thought, as soon as Grandma spoke and beamed.

This was because – lovely as my Grandma is, in a straightforward, no-nonsense, ultra-practical way – I have *never* heard her speak with an exclamation mark at the end of a sentence, and I have *never* known her to beam girlishly.

Something here was very weird indeed...

"I thought you were on a day trip thing today?" I pointed out, as my brain tried to figure out what was going on.

Rowan (still clutching her useless cookbook), Dad (thankfully decent in an old T-shirt and jeans by now), Linn (still in her smart work gear of neat black trousers and black fitted top, before she changed into her casual, lounging-about-the-house outfit of identical neat black trousers and black fitted top) looked just as flummoxed as I felt.

"Yes, we did go to Brighton today..." Grandma twinkled.

Yikes – my Grandma *never* twinkles.

"…and we had a lovely time. A very lovely time indeed."

Uh-oh – now she was twinkling in Stanley's direction and he was twinkling – in a hairy-eared way – back in hers.

"Tell them," Stanley beamed at her.

The beaming, the twinkling … it was making me totally shaky.

"Well, to get to the point," said Grandma, suddenly sounding much more like Grandma, "Stanley asked me to marry him today, and I said yes."

Surprise and shock and nerves have different effects on everybody. Right then, I wanted to do what Dad and Linn and Rowan and Tor and Sandie and Rolf and Winslet were doing and whoop and hug and bark at Grandma and Stanley, but all I could think of was that I had to go for a wee *immediately*. ("Nervous bladder", Grandma informed me later.)

Once I'd got that sorted out (the weeing immediately bit), I found myself staring in the bathroom mirror as I wiped my hands with a cerise towel, listening to the laughing and whooping and barking going on downstairs, and tried to fathom why I suddenly felt so super-sad, at the same time as being super-happy.

Of course, I realized, as an invisible light bulb flickered on above my head. *Someone's missing...*

In two seconds I'd be downstairs, joining in the laughing etc., but a Very Important Person was missing from the family celebrations.

Mum – where are you...?

Chapter 3

YAK, YAK, YAK, YAK, YAK...

After the long, hot, sticky day, a deliciously cool breeze was currently slithering its way through both my open bedroom window and the tilted skylight above my bed. Somewhere in the dark, a furry, four-legged something let out a contented, dreamy snuffle.

In the sudden stillness, I felt myself drifting away to Planet Zzzzz...

And then Sandie started up again.

"It's *soooo* lovely! Isn't it, Ally? Isn't it lovely?" her voice drifted over, from the vicinity of the blow-up mattress on my bedroom floor.

"Yes, it's lovely, Sandie," I mumbled into my pillow, desperate to get some serious snoozing in after such an emotionally charged day. Worrying about towels, being delirious about Grandma's news, missing Mum ... it had really taken it out of me. (OK, maybe not the towel business, so much.)

And another thing, I didn't have a clue what Sandie was currently finding so lovely. Since tonight's spontaneous engagement party had ended and we'd come to bed, Sandie had gushed on (and on) about the loveliness of many, *many* things. At first, I felt so buzzy that I was quite up for sitting in bed and excitedly discussing Grandma's wow of an announcement etc., etc., but an hour later, the only thing I wanted was to get some lovely sleep. Sandie hadn't even taken the hint when I switched the light off – she just kept happily waffling on.

Here's a sample of the various lovely things that Sandie had found to talk about this evening:

- Grandma and Stanley getting married.
- Weddings in general.
- The idea of old people finding true love.
- The idea of finding true love with Billy. (Urgh! *Spare* me...)
- Michael and Harry from next door, who came to join us in the celebrations.
- The vast tub of Häagen Dazs ice-cream that Michael and Harry brought through with them, as well as the champagne (which me and Sandie were allowed a thimbleful of).
- The pizzas Dad sent out for, since it was a special occasion. (Hurrah! We were spared Rowan's Fishy Rice Gloop!)

- The cool breeze wafting through the window.
- The fact that Grandma forgave Rowan for dyeing all the towels pink. (Course, all that might change on Monday, once Grandma came to her senses...)
- Sandie's brand new baby sister back at home.
- Her brand new baby sister's diddy widdle toes and fingers.
- Linn when she smiles. (And she'd smiled all night – quick, pass the sunglasses, someone might get blinded!)
- Billy's smile.
- Alexandra Palace (visible out my bedroom window) being all lit up tonight for some fancy do or other.
- The way Billy's eyes light up when he smiles.
- Billy's freckles.
- Billy's entire God-like being.
- Billy's nose.

No, I'm not joking with that last one. This, apparently, was what Sandie was currently raving on about.

"It's like it's long and straight, but still turns up really cute at the end. Have you noticed that, Ally?"

"No ... I haven't noticed how cute Billy's nose is," I mumbled some more into the pillow.

"Well, why did you say it was lovely just then?"

"I ... I dunno," I shrugged wearily into my pillow, just willing her to suddenly feel as tired as I did.

Cue a second's silence.

"You know, even my mum says Billy's nose is cute," Sandie continued with a giggle, sounding bright as a button, despite the fact that midnight was a long, *long* distant memory.

Ho hum.

I could tell there was no point trying to ignore Sandie when she was all hyper like this, so with a sigh, I flopped around on to my back and stared up at the stars dotting the inky-blue sky through the skylight. And anyway, in the last week since she'd been dating Billy, Sandie had been so bouncing-off-the-walls, blissed-out happy that it would be just plain *mean* of me not to seem interested, or be chuffed for her.

Nope, no matter how much I wanted to barf at the idea of my two best mates kissing, I had to be a good friend and be prepared to talk about it. Even if it killed me.

"You know, it's weird how your mum and dad have taken to Billy, isn't it?" I mused.

"Yeah, they've always been so funny about the idea of me having a boyfriend, haven't they?"

Too *right* they've been funny about the idea of

Sandie having a boyfriend. Until very recently, Mr and Mrs Walker were funny about my best friend having a *life*. They treated Sandie like a cross between a four year old and a crystal ornament. I think they were in total denial that she was actually thirteen years old and went to secondary school. (Exhibit 1: those *Little Mermaid* pyjamas her mum bought her; exhibit 2: her parents flipping the TV channel when there were ads for sanitary towels on, in case the ads shocked her or something; exhibit 3: Sandie always had to hide her teen mags from her parents like they were rude, nudey mags or something.) You know, me and her, we seriously thought her parents wouldn't let her have a boyfriend till she was at *least* 36.

"It's all because Billy helped out when your mum was having her baby, isn't it?" I pointed out.

"Hmm, I guess so…"

Oh, yeah – Billy was very impressive when Mrs Walker went into labour early last weekend, what with phoning for an ambulance and talking her through what she needed to do. Pity he ruined it all by fainting when it finally occurred to him that this was real life and not just something happening on TV.

Still it did the trick, and Mr and Mrs Walker became eternally grateful to him; *so* grateful that they were willing to accept him as boyfriend material for their precious little daughter.

Speaking of precious little daughters…

"Do you think 'cause they've got Bobbie now, your parents are going to get all wrapped up in *her*, and lay off *you*?" I asked Sandie.

"That's what I'm banking on!" Sandie giggled, her grin radiating through the darkness.

"Hey, you were so fazed when you first heard that your mum was pregnant, remember?"

"Uh-huh," Sandie replied.

"But now, it looks like it could be the best thing that ever happened to you!"

"I know!"

We were both quiet for a minute or three, probably the same thoughts ping-ponging around in our minds; that time a few months ago when Sandie went slightly I've-had-my-personality-transplanted-by-aliens odd on me, all because she was upset at the idea of her mum and dad having another junior Walker and maybe not loving her so much. It's funny how things that you dread can sometimes turn out for the best, isn't it?

And *then* I started wondering to myself what it must be like for Sandie; i.e., what it must feel like to be thirteen and have a new sister – a whole new person – suddenly land in your life and turn your entire family upside down. I mean, when you're younger, it's easier to handle new arrivals, somehow. Like when Tor was born, I worried for a while that I might have to share my new bike with him, but once Dad reassured me that that wasn't going to happen, my eight-year-old head totally accepted my little brother. But I don't know how easy it would be to get my head around now, now that I'm so used to my world being the way it is. Which is why I was all of a sudden really proud of Sandie for handling it so well.

"You know, you're totally handling this whole sister thing really well, Sand," I said out loud, since there's no point in just *thinking* a compliment and not letting other people know about it, is there?

No reply. Just a contented, dreamy snuffle, that was definitely of the human – rather than furry, four-legged – variety.

"Night, night, Sand!" I whispered, turning over and snuggling down into my soft pillow.

"*Snurfle*," replied Winslet instead, trampolining her way on to the bed and frantically licking my face like it was coated with gravy.

Yum.

I'd probably end up having dreams of Grandma gliding up the aisle, surrounded by beautiful flowers, and with the scent of smelly doggy breath filling the air...

Chapter 4

TWO FEET ARE COMPANY, THREE'S A CROWD...

"Hee, hee, hee, hee!"

"Heh, heh, heh, heh!"

Urgh, urgh, urgh, urgh...

The hee-hee stuff – that was Sandie giggling. The heh-heh stuff – that was Billy, sniggering. The *urgh* stuff – that was me inwardly groaning, wishing I wasn't sitting alongside the cooing lovebirds like a big, fat lemon.

"Look at it, it's *huge*, Billy!" Sandie pointed straight in front of her, giggling some more.

"It's *not* huge! It's just that yours is so *small*! How can it *be* that small? It's abnormal!"

"Oh, *you*!" snickered Sandie, gently slapping Billy's arm. "You're so *silly*!"

They were speaking about each other's feet, by the way, both of them stretching out a leg each in front of them on the bench and pressing trainers together in mid-air to compare foot sizes. Billy's one chunky Nike trainer *did* dwarf Sandie's dainty red-and-white baseball shoe, but it was hardly the comedy sketch of the century.

"Ally, come on – *you* put your foot up too!" Sandie urged me.

"Uh, no – it's OK," I shrugged. I mean, why would they want my great big lemon of a foot joining in their game? You know that old saying: "Two feet are company, three's a crowd…"

"Aw, go on, Al!" said Billy. "It'll be a laugh!"

I leant forward, looking past Sandie and fixing Billy with a narrow-eyed glare, which translated as, "You *are* kidding, me, right?" I could tell Billy got the message from the way he grinned goofily at me, wriggled about in his seat awkwardly and then looked off into the distance at Winslet and Rolf who were currently wrestling for possession of a stick, while ignoring Billy's yappity poodle Precious.

"What?" Sandie blinked, gazing first at me and then at Billy.

"Nothing," I said, faking a smile, as I suddenly remembered the resolution I'd made in bed last night about trying (really, *really* hard) to be happy for them both.

That was going to be tough, though, specially if it meant my two best friends were now best friends with each *other* and not with *me*. The changes that was going to bring were going to be pretty hard to get used to. For example: normally on Saturday nights when Sandie stays over she just tootles back to her own house after breakfast on Sunday. She leaves me to gather up the dogs (not hard – they're usually sitting at the door with their leads in their mouths from the crack of dawn) and head up to the park at Alexandra Palace for my weekly yakking session with Billy.

But not today.

Today, Sandie came along too, after making us late (Winslet and Rolf set up a howling protest at the delay), 'cause she decided to change her T-shirt three times and couldn't get her fringe blow-dried to perfection. All for Billy's sake, *natch*. The thing is, why did she feel like she had to make an impression? She was already officially going out with him, wasn't she? Did she think he'd chuck her just 'cause she was wearing the wrong colour T-shirt, or because a tuft of hair on the left hand side of her fringe was going a bit boingy? Hey, Billy's shallow (and I should know), but he's not *that* shallow...

And ever since we'd arrived at the park, Sandie and Billy had done nothing but snigger and beam bashfully at one another. I wouldn't have minded, but I'd really fancied having a chat – just me and

Billy – about what was going on with him and Sandie. He'd done an amazing job of avoiding being on his own with me all week, which was down to sheer embarrassment, I suppose. That, and the fact that he knew I'd tease him mercilessly if I got him on his own. (My guess about him being embarrassed was proved the second he saw me and Sand walking up the hill towards him with the dogs. His face was basically one huge blush with a baseball cap stuck on top.)

"Oh, hey, Billy – got some big news," I started to say chattily, knowing that changing the subject (fast) was the only way to stop these two prattling lovey-dovey slush at each other while comparing their knees or their pinkies or their elbows or something.

"Oh, yeah? What's that?" he replied, leaning forward, but not glancing my way (like the big, embarrassed coward that he was).

"Grandma's getting married."

That made him spin his baseball cap round my way pretty smartish…

"Nah! Who's she getting married to?"

Oh, good *grief*. Did Mr and Mrs Walker *realize* they were letting their daughter date someone with the IQ of a particularly thick slug?

"The president of Russia," I replied sarkily.

"Huh?" he blinked at me in confusion.

"Billy – do those two brain cells of yours ever get lonely rattling around together inside your skull?" I asked him pointedly.

"Her gran's marrying Stanley," Sandie prompted him, helping those two brain cells out a little bit.

"I knew *that*! *Course* I knew that!" Billy waffled, wrinkling his nose up as if he'd just been fooling around and putting on the dense act. (He hadn't been – trust me.)

"Oh, *look*, Ally!" Sandie gasped, sounding about as delighted as if someone had just poured a bundle of kittens in her lap. "He's doing that cute turning-up thing with his nose!"

Oh, good grief times *ten*... You know what I needed here? A dollop of hard-hearted cynicism to counteract the unbearable slushy-gushiness I was now witnessing.

And when it comes to hard-hearted cynicism, I knew the very girl...

"You know what it's like? It's like Martians stole their brains and replaced them with Fishy Rice Gloop!" I sighed.

"Fishy Rice Gloop?" Kyra repeated, baffled.

"Well, some kind of mush, whatever," I shrugged, which was pretty pointless 'cause Kyra couldn't see me do it, since she was lounging at home in her room and I was standing in a wee-wee-scented phone box in Priory Road.

A little old lady hovering outside the phone box was currently staring a hole in my head, while rattling the coins in her hand to let me know she was getting impatient.

"Duh!" Kyra's sarky tone replied. "That's what happens when people start going out together, Ally! It's just the way it is!"

This conversation was *not* going the way I had intended. After as much coy, eye-batting, hand-holding fluffiness as I could stand from Sandie and Billy, I'd dragged my reluctant dogs out of the park, and stuffed a pound coin in the first phone box I came across, desperate to hear a voice of reason. Or failing that, Kyra's voice.

"But it's horrible!" I squeaked in protest. "I mean, why can't they just be like that in private, without witnesses? Why can't they just be their normal selves in front of me?"

The old woman was now gazing in vague disgust in the direction of my feet. I glanced down and saw Rolf chewing on a horrible old cigarette packet, while Winslet was amusing herself by bending double and licking her bum.

"That's because neither of them are feeling very

normal right now!" I listened to Kyra state wearily, as if she was explaining something very simple to someone extremely stupid.

"But I don't get it!" I moaned, crouching down and trying to drag the grimy cardboard packet out of Rolf's jaws. (I just left Winslet to it – I didn't really want to be growled at for interrupting her downstairs wash-and-brush-up.)

"Listen, Al," Kyra yawned maddeningly from the other end of the phone line, "you don't *get* it 'cause you've never felt loved-up like Sandie and Billy do right now. Face it, girl – you're jealous."

"I am *not* jealous!"

"Are too."

"Am not!"

"Are too."

"Am not!"

"Are too, are too, are too!"

"Am not, am not, am *not*!"

Sitting on my haunches near the smelly floor of the phone box, with my two dogs doing less-than-lovely things and an old lady giving me the evil eye, I suddenly felt like a total loser.

"Got to go – someone's waiting to use the phone..." I mumbled, straightening up.

"Aw, don't go in a huffle puffle, Al!" Kyra's faint voice drifted from the receiver as I went to hang up. "I was only winding you up! Can't you take a—"

No, I couldn't take a joke. Not when I knew she was right – jealous was exactly what I was feeling and I *hated* to admit it...

Chapter 5

CONFETTI-A-GO-GO

OK – what I said before about being jealous: don't go jumping to the wrong conclusion. I was not (repeat *not*) jealous of Sandie dating Billy 'cause I fancied him or something.

Actually, let me confirm that: I DID NOT AND DO NOT FANCY BILLY!! EXCLAMATION MARK!!!

It took ages to get home from the phone box with Rolf and Winslet, seeing as they were determined to stop and sniff every wall, tree, lamppost and blade of grass peeking between the paving stones. But at least that gave my worrisome mind plenty of time to work out what exactly I *was* jealous of. And the answer to that was...

a) I was jealous of Sandie going out with Billy, in case he ended up wanting to spend all his free time with her, and not with me.

b) I was jealous of Billy going out with Sandie, for exactly the same reason.

c) I was jealous of anyone in the world who

happened to be loved-up, while I was a date-free zone.

d) I was jealous of anyone in the world who had a mum they could see anytime they wanted, even if it *was* a mum who made you wear a vest ten months of the year (Sandie's), or a mum who had a bug-eyed fit if you left a soggy towel on the bathroom floor (Billy's).

Urgh. I was a raging torrent of jealousy and I knew *nothing* anyone could say or do was going to make me feel any better today. Although stuffing an entire family-sized bag of nachos in my mouth at one sitting might help take the edge off my gloom a little bit. And I was sure there was a bag at the back of the cupboard in the kitchen...

"...OK, so we could stick a banner up here," I heard Linn say, as me, Rolf and Winslet padded up to our house, "with '*Congratulations, Irene and Stanley!*' written on it!"

"Yeah, but let's make that too," Rowan replied, gazing up at the little tiled, wooden arch that overhung our front doorstep. "I don't want one of those ready-printed ones you can order out of wedding mags."

"Oh, God, no. If we're going to make all the decorations, then we might as well do that as well. And Grandma would like the personal touch."

"And we could make it match the style of the streamers and the garlands inside the house!"

"Well, we'd better come up with a theme, then."

"Yeah…" Rowan nodded her head thoughtfully, as she and Linn stood side-by-side.

It was such an amazing sight – my two sisters having a perfectly normal discussion, and not bickering for once – that I stood at the gate and watched them for a second, just marvelling at them. Like the World Cup, or the Olympics, or a leap year, or an eclipse, this wasn't something you got to see every day. It was so unexpected that it even startled me into forgetting my jealousy and nacho pangs.

Then Rolf gave me away by barking like a mad thing at a passing butterfly, and Rowan and Linn spun around and caught me gawping.

"What're you doing?" I asked, pretending I didn't know so that I didn't look like some gawping freak just standing there.

"Planning the decorations for Grandma's reception," said Linn, turning my way to reveal a super-efficient clipboard tucked in the nook of her arm.

Last night, Dad and the rest of us were quite chuffed when Grandma announced to us that having her wedding reception at ours was what she'd really, really like. But personally, I thought that – sweet as it sounded – maybe Grandma had just said that 'cause she'd got a teeny bit giddy and sentimental after a few glasses of champagne. Maybe she'd wake up today and realize that holding a wedding reception in the Crouch End equivalent of London Zoo was a very bad idea indeed (all the guests would be picking out cat hairs from the wedding cake). And as for agreeing to let *us* lot sort out the decorations for the do ... well, I was seriously doubting Grandma's sanity now. Wasn't she listening when Tor suggested excitedly last night that he'd cut out lots of home-made confetti for the wedding – in the shape of dinosaurs?

"Sugar plums!" said Rowan suddenly, her eyebrows zooming up towards her fringe. (The fringe was looking much more sensible today, but the rest of her hair wasn't, since she'd got it knotted up in pink foam bendy roller things. She must be doing that to get ringlets or something. Right? *Right*? *Please* tell me those things aren't her latest fashion statement...)

"What *about* sugar plums?" Linn frowned at her, but still scribbled it down on her clipboard anyway.

"Well, that could be our theme for the banners and stuff!" Rowan gushed.

"Yeah, but what *are* sugar plums?" I asked, unhooking Rolf and Winslet's leads and letting them lollop into the house in search of cats to scare and lick. "Are they an actual *thing*?"

"Well, they must be, mustn't they?" Ro shrugged. "Or there wouldn't be a Sugar Plum Fairy in *The Nutcracker* ballet."

"But isn't that just made-up?" I said, wrinkling my nose at my scatty sister. "Like the Tooth Fairy?"

"What *about* the Tooth Fairy?" came Tor's voice, as he appeared in the hall, with a pair of scissors in one hand and a practically life-size paper cut-out of a stegosaurus (his favourite dinosaur) in the other. I hoped for Grandma's sake that this wasn't a sample of the promised confetti, but I had a sneaking suspicion that it was...

"Um, someone Ally knows is getting a tooth out, and is hoping the Tooth Fairy will leave her some money under the pillow tonight for it," Linn lied expertly, for the sake of Tor's innocence.

"Well, Ally's friend's silly," Tor announced, coming and joining us on the front path.

"Why?" Linn asked him.

"'Cause the Tooth Fairy doesn't exist..."

And with that, he was off chasing after a butterfly fluttering by, wafting his paper stegosaurus in
the air after it.

Linn, me and Rowan stared at each other in
surprise for a second. (Tor *always* turns out to be
smarter than we give him credit for.) Then Linn
shrugged and got quickly back to business,
scribbling the words "sugar" and "plum" off her
pad, since it was obvious that none of us knew
what a sugar plum was meant to look like, if it
existed at all.

"And we'll have to work out what we're wearing
too!" Rowan announced.

"To the *wedding*?" I checked with her, never sure
what direction Rowan's dippy mind would take next.

"Of *course* to the wedding!" Linn answered
instead. "We're bridesmaids, remember? Keep up,
Ally!"

"But ... but isn't it a bit early to go planning all
these decorations and outfits and stuff? Grandma
only just told us last night that she was getting
married!"

"Ally – didn't you *hear* the rest of what
Grandma and Stanley were saying?!" said Linn,
staring at me, aghast.

"What?" I asked, bamboozled. What had I
missed?

"They're getting married in *two weeks*, Al!" Ro grinned at me.

"They said that at their time of life, there was no point waiting around," Linn continued, "and Stanley had already checked and found out there was a cancellation at the local registry office!"

Yikes. I couldn't have been more stunned if Linn had confessed to a secret desire to have Rowan do a makeover on her.

The looming wedding date: that must have got mentioned while I was upstairs in the loo having my nervous bladder moment and thinking about Mum.

Well, I guess that solved a problem floating around in my worrisome head. We had no way of contacting Mum, anyway, but if the wedding was only a fortnight away, then there'd be no chance to somehow play detective and track her down with the news, wherever she currently happened to be in the world. So I bit my lip and decided silently that I should put thoughts of her out of my mind and enjoy this whole wedding doodah, whatever...

Of course, there was one other very *large* thing to worry about.

"Um, Ro..." I began, "you won't be, um ... *designing* our bridesmaid outfits, will you?"

"Oooh! I hadn't *thought* about actually *designing* them!" she gasped. "What a brilliant idea, Ally!"

Linn narrowed her eyes at me and sighed a sigh that was all too easy to translate.

Yeah, I know... Why didn't I keep my dumb mouth shut...?

Chapter 6

SANDIE'S DIFFERENT DIFFERENCE

Anyone watching us from the other side of the road might have wondered what invisible thing it was that me, Rolf and Winslet were staring at so intently on the pavement.

The invisible thing wasn't *actually* invisible (it'd only seem that way if you weren't right up close) – it was a small snail, snailing its way along the paving stones at surprisingly high speed for something with no feet to propel it. In the time that me, Rolf and Winslet had sat on the bench outside the community centre, it had got all the way from the bus stop and was now nearly at the crumpled-up crisp packet by my left foot.

"Wow!" I hear you cry in amazement. (Or not...)

Look, it was a very, very hot day and yes, the three of us *were* kind of bored and listless as we hung around waiting for Tor to come out of his summer arty-crafty class thing. Anyway, that's my excuse for me and the pooches mindlessly staring at the snail, even if it looked kind of weird to all the mums and dads and minders who were hovering around waiting to collect their own small people. (There was a shy-looking Muslim woman in one of those *hijab* headscarves standing right outside the door, I noticed – I wondered if she was the mum of Amir, Tor's buddy. Not that I was going to introduce myself – it was pretty clear by Amir's reaction to our family on the few occasions he'd been round our house that he thought we were all certifiably crazy, so if he'd said as much to his mum then I didn't suppose she'd exactly try and *hug* me if I said hello or anything. She was more likely to shoo me away...)

Grandma usually came to collect Tor, but she'd volunteered me to do it today, 'cause she had wedding-y stuff to sort out, she said. ("Tor *did* offer to make our invitations, but I have a feeling that some of our friends might be a little confused by the stegosaurus potato prints he wanted to do," said Gran, as she headed off to WHSmith in Wood Green to buy a pack of sensible, stegosaurus-free, ready-printed cards.)

Anyway, I didn't mind picking up Tor – I'd arranged to meet Salma and her small bundle of relations round the caff in Priory Park straight after.

"It's fast, isn't it?" said Tor, appearing magically by my side and joining in our snail-staring session.

"Yeah, s'pose… So, anyway, fancy going and getting an ice-cream?" I asked him, as my mind shot off at a tangent and imagined how deliciously cooling and tempting it would be to rub a Magnum bar all over my over-heating self right at that moment. (I might look like a total nutter with melted chocolate all over me, of course. That would *really* frighten Amir off. Just then, I spotted him on the other side of the road, whispering something to his concerned-looking mum while they hurried away.)

"Ice-cream? Yeah!" Tor nodded with a grin a mile wide.

"How's Amir doing?" I asked Tor, as I gathered up the dogs' leads and tried a friendly wave across the road in the direction of Amir and his mum. She gave me a polite but worried nod in return, obviously concerned about our family's apparent interest in all things black magic. Which wasn't the case at all – there was a perfectly simple explanation for all the supposedly weird stuff Amir had witnessed round our place recently. For example, OK, so he might not have seen any girl dress as eccentrically as Rowan back in his own country, but Ro hadn't *meant* to alarm him with her mental fashion statements. And then there was the time Tor hypnotized his pet pigeon, but there's nothing really weird about *that*, is there? (Er, funnily enough, that *does* look a bit weird now that I've written it down...)

"He's OK," Tor shrugged, picking up the snail and gently plopping it on to the much more snail-friendly grass on the verge behind the bench. (Actually, I wasn't sure whether he was talking about the snail now or Amir.)

"And how's Amir's English coming on?"

As I asked Tor that, I stood up, brushing the back of my bare thighs for splinters.

"Taught him a new word today."

"Uh-huh? What was that, then?"

"'Stegosaurus'."

Hmm. *That* was certainly a very useful word to add to a refugee kid's vocabulary. He'd get a lot of use out of "stegosaurus", seeing as the whole of Crouch End is awash with them. I *don't* think.

"'Stegosaurus' ... cool," I nodded slowly. "OK, so let's go get that ice-cream."

"Oh, Tor! Hold on a second!" a voice called out, stopping us in our tracks.

I turned to see a very pretty woman, wearing jeans, slip-on trainers and a white cheesecloth shirt come hurrying towards my brother with a rolled-up paper something in her hands. It must be Miss Woods, the arty-crafty teacher Tor liked so much.

"You forgot this!" Miss Woods panted, holding the something out to him.

"Hi, I'm Ally. I'm Tor's sister," I said, unable to drag my eyes away from Tor's teacher's amazing hair. Rowan's got a poster in her room by this old-fashioned ("Pre-Raphaelite!") painter bloke called Rossetti, and the girl in the poster has the exact same hair as this Miss Woods, all mad red ringlets tumbling over her shoulders and down her back. Only the girl in the 1800-and-something painting didn't have bits of her hair pinned back with a couple of blue and yellow plastic clothes pegs.

I can't have been too subtle in my gawping – Miss Woods's hands immediately fluttered up to her hair and yanked the pegs out.

"Silly me!" she giggled. "I forgot I had these in! I lost my scrunchie somewhere and these were all I could find to keep my hair at bay! Anyway, hi, Ally! Hey, Tor – are you going to show your sister your brilliant drawing?"

Beaming with pride, my pink-cheeked little bruv unrolled the paper and held it up for me to see. It consisted of two smiley people, standing in a field of crayon-green grass and daisies.

"Oh, Tor – Grandma will love this!" I praised him, as my eyes wandered over the drawing, and recognized one smiley person as Grandma, from the neat little specs it was wearing. "And *that* looks *exactly* like Stanley!"

I think it might have been the hair sprouting out of the ears that gave it away.

"We're going for an ice-cream now." Tor blushed sweetly in Miss Woods's direction, completely ignoring my compliment.

You know, when he said that, it was almost like he was half-inviting her along…

"Are you? That sounds lovely!" she smiled at us both. "Well, I won't keep you guys. See you next time, Tor!"

As Miss Woods waved and went back in the building, Tor stood staring after her.

"Ice-cream?!" I reminded him, handing him Winslet's lead, and letting her drag him along the pavement.

You know something? It was like he didn't even hear me.

Bizarre…

"I think Tor's got a crush on his summer school teacher," I told Salma, as I joined her on the bench just outside the fenced off, dog-free zone of the toddler paddling pool in Priory Park.

I'd just gone to the loos at the back of the café there and filled an old, empty margarine tub I'd taken with me with water. As soon as I put it on the ground, Rolf and Winslet started slurping out of it like they'd been in the Sahara desert for a fortnight.

"Aw, that's so cute!" smiled Salma, passing back my (dripping) Twister ice-cream that she'd been holding for me. "Why do you think that?"

"Just the way he went mushy when she talked to him this afternoon," I explained, quickly licking the dribbles from my Twister before they dripped all over my hand. "*And* he's all chuffed 'cause she let him in on a secret today!"

"Which was?" Salma asked, holding back her long, dark hair and licking the bottom of her own fast-melting Solero.

"Well, on the way round here he told me that when she'd first come over and looked at the picture he'd done –" I nodded my head in the direction of Tor's rolled-up piece of artwork sticking out of my rucksack beside me "– she apparently pointed to all the daisies and said that *that* was her first name!"

"Daisy?" Salma repeated.

"Uh-huh. Daisy Woods," I nodded. "Pretty, isn't it? But it's like Tor thinks it's a total honour or something to be told that!"

"Aww, bless him!" Salma cooed, staring off at my soggy brother, who was currently being ganged up on by Salma's three-and-a-half-year-old monsters – er, twin sisters and niece, I mean. Tor was getting splashed in the pool so hard by the giggling trio of trouble that his T-shirt and shorts were soaking. "Hey, isn't he looking grown-up all of a sudden?"

It's not hard looking grown-up when you tower over legions of teenies like Julia, Rosa and Laurel, all shrieking and sploshing about in the ten-centimetre deep water of the pool. But I knew what Salma meant; I mean, Tor was always the responsible "big boy" whenever Salma's little monsters were around (giving me and Sal time to gossip), but yeah, all of a sudden he *did* seem to be looking less of a kid, and more of a lad.

"I guess he has changed a bit recently," I had to agree with her, wondering if it was the fact that Tor seemed to have shot up in the last few hot weeks, just like the flowers (and the weeds) in our back garden. Or maybe it was that combined with the fact that he seemed to be having his first junior crush.

Wow … our gorgeous little brother not being the baby of the family any more – I wasn't sure if I liked that idea…

"Hey, I tell you who *else* has changed recently," said Salma, unaware that I'd suddenly come over all soppy.

"Who?"

"Sandie."

"You think?" I turned and frowned at her.

"Well, I saw her earlier this afternoon – she was coming out of the library when I was going in with the brats," shrugged Salma, "and she just seemed ... different."

"Different how?" I asked, wondering why Sandie hadn't got back to me after I'd left a "hello" message with her mum this morning.

"I dunno. Like she's ... taller ... or smilier ... or *glowier* or something," said Salma, making up words in an effort to describe Sandie's new different difference.

"Or maybe just kind of ... more confident?" I suggested, pretty sure now I knew what Salma was getting at.

"Confident! Yeah, exactly!" Salma nodded. "Isn't that weird?"

It sure was. Sandie could win prizes in shy competitions, if there were such things. Well, normally. But then the last week ... you couldn't quite see her jumping on the tables in Burger King in Wood Green High Street and belting out a version of "...Baby One More Time", but she *definitely* seemed a noticeable shade less shy. And we all knew why *that* was, of course.

"Guess it's all because of her and Billy being together," I shrugged, still vaguely bamboozled by the whole concept of the two of them being an item.

"Yeah, definitely. You should have *seen* the way they were all giggly today when I bumped into them."

Ah … so there was my answer; the reason why Sandie hadn't returned my phone call. She was hanging out with Billy again today. (And it *must* be true love if Sandie had managed to get allergic-to-books-Billy over the threshold of the local library.)

Suddenly, that wibbly pang of jealousy twanged in my chest all over again, and I really didn't appreciate that.

"Hey, what's Tor doing now?" Salma asked, pointing in the direction of the paddling pool.

I glanced over, and through the swarms of soggy, happy toddlers I saw that the mini-tornadoes had now left Tor alone and started splashing each other, while Tor sat at the edge of the pool, turning his head and talking to … thin air.

"I have absolutely no idea," I muttered, "but he's been doing it a *lot* lately."

Aw, well – my brother might have been going mad in front of my very eyes, but at least it took my mind off all that stupid, pointless twanging jealousy stuff…

Chapter 7

CARTWHEELS AND CORNY LOVEY-DOVEYNESS

"Look, I'm sorry, but I'm not listening to any more excuses. This has gone on *far* too long as it is."

I could hear Grandma's raised voice, as me, Tor and the dogs hovered outside the front door. Yikes – she sounded in a stern mood. Who was at the receiving end of that, I wondered? Was it human or animal? Was she sniping at Rowan for frittering away a week's pocket money on yet another set of fairy lights for her room? Or had Colin the cat made a nest in the nice warm pile of ironing in the laundry basket, like he always tried to do when Grandma wasn't looking? Whichever, it was just as well me and Tor had paused on the front doorstep, stopping to take off his sopping wet T-shirt and shorts so that he didn't leave a dripping trail of puddles all down the hall. (*That* certainly wouldn't improve Grandma's current mood, I didn't think.)

"OK," I nodded at Tor, opening the door and letting him and Rolf and Winslet bolt inside.

I was just wringing out my brother's T-shirt and shorts over the unwatered, drooping geraniums in the flowerpot by the doormat when I heard the tail end of Grandma's conversation, which she *wasn't* having with either Rowan, or a randomly badly behaved pet, by the looks of it.

"...no, I'm *not* being harsh – I'm just being honest!" she frowned at the floor as she spoke into the phone. "Oh! Someone's just come in! Listen, we'll ... we'll discuss this later. All right? Bye."

The someone coming in was Tor, of course, and the shock of seeing him swoop by her in just a pair of damp Thomas the Tank Engine pants and trainers soon put paid to Grandma's terse conversation with whoever.

"He got soaked in the pool at Priory Park – it was Salma's lot's fault," I said by way of an explanation, as I stepped into the hall with his now wrung-out and tangled pile of clothes and shut the door behind me.

"Right..." nodded Grandma, looking slightly preoccupied.

"Um, did you get all your wedding stuff sorted?" I asked her, pointing to the phone.

"Oh, yes," Grandma replied, after a moment's

hesitation. "Well, nearly. There's such a lot to see to, and such a lot of complications."

"Sounded like it!" I said cheerfully, pointing at the phone again, and thinking of the narked exchange she'd just had.

"That!" Grandma raised her eyebrows sharply at me. "Well, that was just something that'll get sorted, same as everything else."

"Salma said that when her mum was getting remarried, she nearly cancelled it all, 'cause it was such a hassle to organize," I chattered, remembering part of the conversation I'd had with my friend earlier, as Grandma led the way through to the kitchen, taking Tor's wet things from me.

"I can understand that!" Grandma laughed wryly, carrying on through the kitchen and out of the back door, with me still following. "Even though Stanley and I want to keep our wedding simple, there still seems so much to do!"

"What about when you married Grandad?" I asked, thinking of one black and white photo in particular on Grandma's mantelpiece. It was of Grandma in a tweed skirt and jacket, wearing a neat little hat and carrying a neat little bouquet of carnations, standing alongside Grandad Miller, who was wearing an over-sized, dark suit with a matching flower in his buttonhole.

"Dear me, Ally, that was such a long time ago, I can hardly remember it!" Grandma smiled, shrugging off her memories in that typically unsentimental way of hers.

If you're looking for fascinating tales of the past, heart-warming reminiscences or anecdotes from the family tree, then you're wasting your time asking someone like Grandma. She's a firm believer in living in the here and now, and would be far happier concentrating on hanging up Tor's wet things on the clothes line like she was doing than ambling down memory lane and sharing her past experiences with me. Still, I wasn't going to let her off the hook that easily. If she didn't want to talk about her *own* wedding, then there was another one she could talk about; one that happened 17 years ago; one that I never tired hearing about...

"Were Mum and Dad nervous the day *they* were getting married?" I asked her.

"I expect so."

"But they were really happy, right?"

"Well, that's the way you're supposed to feel when you're getting married, or there's no point doing it," Grandma replied breezily. "Can you pass me *that* over, Ally, dear?"

You know, when Grandma isn't in the mood to talk about something, she is very good at stubbornly, annoyingly skirting around it. Trying to figure out a better way to restart this conversation, I watched her fish out another couple of pegs from the bag I was now holding out to her. Her fingers randomly pulled out a yellow and a blue one, I couldn't help noticing – the same as Daisy Woods had had clamped in her hair today. Which reminded me...

"Oh, hold on – Tor made you something at his class today," I told her.

"Did he?" Grandma frowned slightly, gazing over in the direction of Tor, who was doing cart-wheels in his pants on the lawn, with Rolf and Winslet barking their appreciation. (Well, at least he wasn't talking to himself for once.)

"It's OK – it's nice; it's a drawing," I hurried to reassure her, knowing that she was probably dread-ing getting a twine 'n' twig soap dish to match her twine 'n' twig toothbrush holder.

I was just about to head into the house and get the drawing to show her, when Dad – home from a hard day's bicycle repairing – ambled out of the back door slowly (a cat that wasn't Colin was winding its way affectionately around Dad's legs) and joined us in the garden, wafting a bundle of coloured leaflets in his hand.

"Hi, Ally Pally! Hi, Irene!" he beamed. "What's

going on with Tor? Has he been playing strip poker with the dogs or something?"

"Aliens stole his clothes!" I beamed back in Dad's direction.

"Ah! Of course!" he laughed, plonking himself down on a deckchair and letting the cat that wasn't Colin bounce up on to his lap and purrily claw at his worn, faded jeans.

"Tor and Salma's little ones were playing in the paddling pool at Priory Park and they all got soaked," Grandma explained more sensibly, as Tor cartwheeled his way past us and over to Dad.

"So I see," said Dad, slapping his hand gently on Tor's damp bum, as my brother ground to a wobbly, upright halt at Dad's side.

"Wassat?" Tor panted, pointing at the leaflets Dad was holding.

"Vouchers for the Russian State Circus," Dad announced. "They're going to be in Ally Pally all week."

"Yeah – me and Tor saw the poster for that, didn't we, Tor?"

Tor nodded hard at me in reply.

"Well, these are special half-price vouchers – some bloke from the circus was handing them out to all the shops in the road today. And since it means the tickets are half-price, I just thought that maybe we could all go tomorrow night. A family night out. All except for Tor, of course…"

"Arghhhh! Not *fair*!" Tor roared, leaping on to Dad and sending the cat that wasn't Colin scarpering for a more relaxing place to, er, relax.

"I'm afraid I'll be too busy with wedding bits and bobs to come, Martin," Grandma excused herself loudly – above the sound of the doorbell ringing and Dad and Tor play-fighting – before disappearing into the house to answer the door.

"Linn can't come either," I yelled above Tor and Dad's whoops and snorts as they did a Death By Tickling duel in the deckchair. "She's going out with her mates."

I knew that even if Linn *hadn't* truly been going out with her mates, she'd have pretended she was. She does love us all – in a strange, well hidden way – but her idea of torture would be hanging out at the circus with us lot. Last time we went, a couple of years ago, a clown sprayed her with foam and made her hair go curly, and then Rowan accidentally stuck her candyfloss to the side of Linn's head. Linn probably still has nightmares about it…

"Hi, Ally!" Sandie's voice suddenly called out. "We were just passing and we thought we'd say hello!"

The "we" was her and Billy, naturally, and they were walking out of the back door and across the grass, holding hands, very *un*naturally.

"Hi, guys!" Dad turned and immediately grinned, when he clocked the hand-holding. "I didn't know *you* two were together!"

Mainly because I hadn't told him. And that was mainly because the whole idea of Sandie and Billy was too ... *icky* to chat with your family about over breakfast or whatever. (It could give a girl indigestion.)

"We've been going out for ten days now, haven't we?" Sandie explained to Dad as she beamed at Billy, who just blushed and beamed back at her, like a silent, blushing, beaming berk.

"Well, well! That's great!" Dad nodded at them both, shooting me a why-didn't-you-say-something? look. Tor, meanwhile, slipped off Dad's lap and went back to cartwheeling, since the conversation had turned from fascinating (i.e. circuses) to boring (i.e. love). "When did this all happen? I mean, how did you two get together?"

"After Billy helped last weekend, when Mum had my baby sister and everything," said Sandie, radiating pride and happiness.

I was just radiating ... I dunno, *embarrassment* at the sight of the two of them together, but I couldn't keep my eyes off Billy, who was avoiding my gaze at all costs, I noticed.

"Great! Well done, Billy, lad!" Dad laughed, reaching over and punching Billy matily on the arm.

"Huhh-ununghhh!" Billy snorted in response. I think he was trying to look pleased or something, but it just came across more like he was choking on a chip at the same time as trying to smile.

"So how *is* your baby sister?" Dad chattered away to Sandie. "What's her name again?"

"Roberta. Bobbie for short. Well, that's what *I'm* going to call her. She's *soooo* cute..."

While Sandie and Dad yakked, I stared hard at Billy, willing him psychically to look over at me. He wouldn't. But I was sure he was aware of my thoughts boring into his head, from the way he was staring down at the ground, growing pinker by the millisecond.

"...and she's got the *teeniest* little toes, hasn't she, Billy?"

Billy grinned and nodded so hard his baseball cap wobbled.

Good grief! This was insane – my best boy mate was turning weirder on me by the second, his current state of corny lovey-doveyness sucking his brain dry of any sense. I mean, why was he letting Sandie do all the talking, as if he'd lost the ability to speak now? And why was he acting so pinkly shy in front of me all of a sudden?

Right that second, I made a decision. Seeing the two of them together like this was just going to make my head go twisty. The only thing for it was to see them separately from now on, since they turned into corny slush-buckets whenever they were together.

Or maybe I shouldn't see either of them for a while, I wondered to myself. *At least not till they come back down to earth from Planet Lurve...*

"...and I've got loads, so you could come too!" I heard Dad say, though I wasn't sure what he was on about.

"Oh, yeah, we'd *love* to come, wouldn't we, Billy?" Sandie replied enthusiastically, taking – eek! – the two money-off circus vouchers that Dad was holding out to her.

"Huhh-ununghhh!" Billy nodded.

"That'll be fun, having Sandie and Billy come along with us to the circus, won't it, Ally Pally?" Dad smiled at me, same as Sandie was now doing.

"Yes," I heard myself fib.

Brilliant. A whole evening of sitting next to my mentally-deranged, love-sick mates, watching them *drooling* over each other.

Pass the sick-bag, please...

Chapter 8

A TUMMY'S WORTH OF BACK-FLIPS...

"Oooh! Little fat ladies! Aren't they sweet?" Rowan cooed, as Tor played with the set of pale blue and gold Russian dolls for sale at the counter, fitting one inside the other.

Luckily, the woman behind the counter didn't seem to mind Tor fooling around with the dolls. That was because...

1) Anyone with a brain could see he was a very considerate, careful kid, and not the sort who'd thud the dolls together so hard they'd chip the paint and ham-fistedly send halves of fat Russian lady dolls clattering on to the sawdust-covered earth floor.

2) His gentle fascination with the dolls was capturing the interest of quite a few people in the crowd during this intermission, and I'm sure the lady behind the desk was rubbing her hands together at the thought of potential customers parting with a few quid for prettily painted Russian dolls rather than just a coffee or a hot dog at the stand next to hers.

3) Tor was snapping together the cheapest of the doll sets – all the more amazing, bigger, shinier, glitzier, more expensive sets were safely stashed on a big set of shelves behind her.

4) The doll-selling lady may well have been too busy gawping at Rowan to even *notice* what Tor was up to. In honour of the whole Russian nation, Rowan had decked herself out in black suede knee-high boots (very comfortable on a hot August evening, I *don't* think), a flouncy dark-blue peasant-style skirt, a red cotton top with short puff sleeves, and – get this – an Alice band covered in fake flowers with lengths of coloured ribbon trailing from it down either side of her head. (She was up half the night sewing that lot on.) For reference, she'd dragged out an art book she'd borrowed – and was long overdue returning – from the school library. The painting she'd shown me last night was of some Russian folk scene from a couple of hundred zillion years ago. I didn't like to tell her that the fourteen-year-old Moscow girl I saw getting interviewed on a schools' documentary programme last term was wearing Levi jeans and a Juventas footie top. I think that *she* was probably more your average teenage Russian girl than the version Rowan was copying from the folk painting...

"Ally..." muttered Tor, pushing the now

snapped-together and completed doll back along the counter and turning to me.

"What?" I bent over to hear him, sussing from his expression that he wanted to say something private.

"That lady," he mumbled, moving his head infinitesimally in front of him, towards a young girl wandering around carrying a tray of ice-cream amongst the crowds. "She was up in the roof."

So she was. Tor had been enraptured by the first half of the circus show, dazzled by the bright lights, the tumbling acrobats, the silky costumes, the stupid antics of the clowns, the jugglers, the wibbly-wobbly but non-falling high-wire walkers, but what seemed to be startling him even more at the moment was seeing all the daring, life-risking performers chuck a T-shirt or something over their spangly costumes and sell choc chip ice-cream and programmes during the break.

"My God, she is gorgeous…" Rowan sighed, as the stunning young ice-cream-selling/tightrope-walking girl passed by. Her hair was pulled up and back in a tight bun and her eyes were accentuated with theatrical, glittery blue eyeshadow (to match the costume hidden under her Russian State Circus red T-shirt) and sweeps of black eyeliner.

Aha! I could spot Rowan's next fashion craze a mile off…

"Going to find Dad," I suddenly heard Tor say, while me and Rowan were both still gawping at the ridiculously amazing cheekbones of the Russian girl.

"Tor…!" I called after him uselessly, but he was already gone. Not that I was too worried – he couldn't go far; the entrance area to the circus tent might have been busy, but it was full of kids and parents and grandparents, and I could see Dad's head of dark cropped curls quite clearly as he stood in the never-ending queue for drinks and nibbles.

However, I didn't know where Sandie and Billy were. Thanks to the god of circus seating, we'd arrived too late to sit all together, and the last I'd seen of my canoodling chums was them holding hands and staring into each other's eyes five rows behind us, just as the lights went down at the start of the performance. For all I knew, they'd spent the whole of the first half sighing at the wondrousness of each other, while some poor Russian trapeze bloke risked life and limb doing a triple somersault without them even noticing…

"Oh, look – Dad's got him," Rowan laughed, and so he had – there was Tor being lifted into the air above people's heads, giggling as Dad's firm grip sent him aeroplaning upwards.

"Dad'll pull a muscle. Have you noticed how big Tor's suddenly getting?" I asked my sis.

"Who's that woman Dad's with? The one laughing up at Tor?" Rowan asked blithely, ignoring my remark. "She's got beautiful hair..."

Tiptoeing myself upwards so I could see what Rowan could see (she had several centimetres' advantage on me, since her boots were high wedges), I caught sight of a bundle of familiar red curls, around a pretty, smiling face.

"That's Daisy," I mumbled, leaning up on Ro's shoulder to keep my balance.

"Daisy?"

"Daisy Woods – Tor's summer school teacher."

"The art club thing he goes to, you mean?" asked Ro, the ribbons on either side of her head jiggling as she talked.

"Yep," I replied. "She's really nice. I think Tor's got a bit of a crush on her!"

"Yeah? Ooh, let's go and meet her, then!" Rowan giggled, yanking me forward into the crowd. "I've got to meet the older woman who's captured the heart of our little bruv!"

Just as we began pushing through the throng, a scratchy announcement came across the tannoy, letting us all know that the second half of the performance would start in two minutes. Almost magically, the crowd began to thin out, streaming back towards the rows and racks of seats in the huge tent.

"Who's your dad chatting up, then?" Billy's voice asked tactlessly, as Sandie and him appeared out of nowhere by our sides, their arms wrapped around each other like they had been strapped together by invisible parcel tape.

Billy might have gone weird on me lately, but I knew what he'd just said was meant to be a joke. Only from where I was standing, it somehow didn't seem too funny to see how smiley and friendly and chatty Dad and Daisy Woods were acting towards one another. It was mad to think that way, I knew – after all, there was Tor, standing beaming with them, and all he'd done was introduce his dad to his teacher. There was nothing wrong with that. It was all absolutely normal and natural and fine, whatever Billy the berk jokingly said.

So why did it make me feel so ... odd?

And then I figured it out. For a split second there, staring at Dad and Daisy Woods, I got the funniest feeling ... that déjà vu people speak about, when something seems spookily familiar. Without me even asking, my brain turned into a search engine, scrawling through my memory banks to work out why exactly this scene was so familiar. And then it found it...

A photo of Dad, all animated, his expression full of excitement and happiness, gazing at a mirror-image expression in a beautiful, smiling face. It was a photo of Mum and Dad at the top of Glastonbury Tor, taken by ten-year-old Linn, while me and Rowan were probably trying to roll down the hill, giggling. That was when Tor was small as a plum, tucked cosily in Mum's womb, unknown to anyone at that point.

But there Tor was now – standing in between our twinkly-eyed Dad and an equally twinkly-eyed Daisy Woods – staring up at the two of them with a smile a mile wide on his face.

"They look like … a family," I suddenly heard Rowan whisper into my ear, and knew her tummy was tumbling like there was a troupe of tiny acrobats back-flipping inside it, same as mine…

Chapter 9

GETTING TO THE BOTTOM OF THE TWINKLING

Twinkling. There was *way* too much of it going on for my liking. First, there was Sandie and Billy twinkling at each other, and now…

"*Please*, Ally!"

"No!"

"Oh, *please*!"

"I'm not going to do it, Ro!"

"Pretty please – with sugar on top!"

"Rowan, you can say pretty please with *nachos* on top, but I'm still not doing it!"

"But you *have* to!"

"Why do *I* have to? Why can't *you* talk to Dad?"

"Because you'll be so much better at it than me! You're so clever, Ally, you'll say it all right! I'd just babble!"

True. But it still wasn't fair to make *me* do the deed.

"I don't care what you say, Ro – I'm *still* not doing it."

Rowan stared mournfully at me, looking like a

sad puppy, specially with her hair in floppy-ear-style bunches like it was today. Any minute now, she was probably going to whine pitifully.

But her sad puppy act wasn't going to change my mind, oh no. She wasn't going to get around me *that* easily.

Uh-uh.

No way.

No way, José.

"Hi Dad..."

OK, so call me a soft touch. Rowan had got her way, and here I was, round at Dad's shop, the day after our night at the circus. And I was round here on a mission, because of a dilemma. And if that makes no sense, then let me explain...

THE DILEMMA: Last night, Dad had seemed way, *way*, way too relaxed with Miss Woods, getting all twinkly-eyed with her, even though they'd only spoken for about a nano-second in the interval. And he hadn't been able to shut up about her after we got back to our seats either. It turned out, he told us, that they had mutual mates in common – Miss Woods knew someone at Dad's line-dancing class. He laughed when he told us that, and said he'd teased her about coming along sometime and joining in all the skipping and yahooing (or whatever it is people *do* at line-dancing). His eyes were as sparkly as the circus lights when he'd spoken about her. This did not seem quite right to me and Rowan. At all.

MY MISSION: To chat to Dad casually, to gain his trust, then sneak in a few questions about Miss Woods to see if he was still all twinkly-eyed about her in the cold light of day. If he wasn't, then hurrah. If he *was*, then ... I dunno. Panic, I suppose.

"Hey, Ally Pally!" Dad smiled at me in surprise, as the bell on the door tinkled as it shut behind me and the dogs. "Come to help me mend a few bikes, have you?"

He was crouched on the floor, fitting a bike chain to a currently wheel-less bike. Little did he know that I was here to try and suss him out; to see if there was the *faintest* possibility that he had the *teeniest* hint of feelings for someone that wasn't Mum. I knew we'd been through all this before a few months ago, when me and both my sisters were *convinced* Dad was seeing someone else, when he *wasn't* – but this time, me and Ro had witnessed real smiles and real twinkles with our own eyes.

"No thanks," I smiled back at Dad, watching as he stood up and rubbed the oil off his hands with an old rag. "I wouldn't want to get my *lovely* outfit dirty."

With that, I swept my hands out to display my paw-print-covered, grubby white T-shirt, unravelling denim cut-offs and most battered pair of trainers (one of which had been lightly chewed by Winslet before I put it on).

"Well, that's quite understandable. So, to what *do* I owe the pleasure of your company, dearest daughter of mine?" Dad asked, putting on an olde worlde BBC-costume-drama voice.

"Um, Rowan sent me to ask you something," I said truthfully.

"Oh, yeah?" muttered Dad distractedly, as he walked backwards from me and stuck an arm into the tiny back workshop to flick the kettle on. (Rolf and Winslet were already snuffling about through there – they knew there was usually a packet of biscuits to be found amongst the cogs and spokes and nuts and bolts and general bike bits).

"Yeah, she asked me to ask you," I continued, remembering what Rowan had coached me to say, "do you think we should put up fairy lights in the garden? For Grandma's wedding reception, I mean?"

("Don't ask about Miss Woods straight away!" Rowan had advised me, just before I'd walked round here. "Lull him into a false sense of security by maybe talking about the wedding and stuff, and then just slip in something about her!")

"Fairy lights in the garden?" Dad nodded enthusiastically. "*That* sounds good! We've got one set already, haven't we? The ones we put on the front door for Christmas. But we'd need more than that. Wonder if there's somewhere you can hire them? Or maybe I could buy some more... I'm sure B&Q are having a half-price summer sale on garden stuff... They open late, don't they? I can't go tonight since it's Wednesday and line-dancing, but maybe I should cycle down there tomorrow after work and check it out..."

As Dad prattled on, he dipped into the back room, and began clattering teacups around. I, meanwhile, was worrying and wondering how to twist the conversation round from fairy lights to Daisy Woods. Stupidly enough, Rowan and I hadn't worked that out beforehand.

"There you go!" said Dad, passing me a steaming mug. "And do you fancy a Digestive? Before the bottomless pits here finish them off?"

He walked back out into the main shop, carrying the biscuits, his own cup of tea, and followed by Rolf and Winslet, crunching like crazy with tell-tale crumbs around their muzzles.

"No, I'm OK," I replied, shaking my head at his

offer. My tummy was too tangled in nervous knots to eat.

"It's going to be fun, this wedding, isn't it?" said Dad, through a mouthful of Digestive. "Are you looking forward to it?"

"Oh, yeah, of course!" I told him. "Only..."

Urgh ... I hadn't meant for that "only" to sneak out.

"Only?" Dad repeated, frowning at me slightly.

"Only ... I wish Mum was going to be here for it."

There. I'd said it. I hadn't said it to anyone in my family before now, because I didn't want to seem like a little black cloud of gloom over Grandma's happy news. And I hadn't confided in my best friends, since two of them (guess who) were too busy kissing each other to worry about what *I* was up to, and the third one (Kyra) was very good for having a laugh with but not much cop when it came to emotions and feelings and stuff.

"Hey..." said Dad, cocking his head to one side and studying me. "Is that upsetting you?"

"A bit," I shrugged.

And with that, Dad stuck his mug down and came over to give me a bear-hug, sending the contents of *my* mug sploshing on to the floor. (I couldn't look down, 'cause my head was nuzzled comfortably into Dad's skinny chest, but I could hear some slurping going on and knew that a doggy hoover was taking care of the spills.)

"I know it's weird not having Mum around for a special occasion like this," I heard Dad say soothingly, as he rocked me gently from side-to-side. "And it's not just you, Ally; I think we're all feeling it…"

(Ooh, this was nice. I was glad I *had* said that "only" now. Being comforted and reassured by Dad was just what I needed, *and* knowing from what he was saying that he missed Mum as much as any of us did. Which meant all that twinkling between him and Miss Woods … well, it hadn't meant anything. It was just a trick of the light and me and Rowan being paranoid morons.)

"…specially Grandma, even though she hasn't admitted it," he carried on, stroking my hair with one hand. "But we've just got to be cheerful for Grandma's sake and try to— oh! Hello!"

Suddenly, at the sound of the bell on the door tinkling, the hair-stroking stopped. As I turned to see who Dad was talking to, his arm was still around my shoulders, but his attention was certainly not on me any more. He was smiling – and *twinkling* – in the direction of the pretty woman pushing a battered old mountain bike in front of her into the shop.

"Sorry – I'm not interrupting, am I?" she smiled, putting one hand up to push the tangle of red curls away from her face.

"No! Not at all!" Dad told her, before turning to me. "You remember Daisy, don't you, Ally?"

"Yes," I nodded, forcing a wibbly-wobbly smile on my face. "Er, hi!"

"Hi, Ally!" Daisy Woods smiled back at me, without a wibble-wobble in sight. "So, Martin ... are you sure you've got time to look at my bike today? I know you said so last night..."

"It's fine! No problem!" Dad grinned, letting go of me and taking hold of the bike handlebars.

"It's just that I don't want to put you out," Daisy Woods said apologetically. "I mean, I could easily come back another day if you're busy..."

"Don't be silly! Why don't you take a seat? It'll only take a minute to fix."

I didn't know *what* exactly Dad had promised to fix for Daisy Woods, but all I knew was that there was so much *twinkling* going on between them that I needed sunglasses to stop my eyes from being dazzled by it.

Uh-oh...

Chapter 10

MARSHMALLOW IS THE NEW BLACK...

If the weirdness I'd just witnessed at the shop wasn't weird enough, there was plenty more going on back home.

"Listen, this is just getting *silly*," I caught Grandma growling into the phone, as me and the dogs bundled through the front door. "Now you listen to me..."

That was weird on two counts: first, Grandma is always very even-tempered; even when she's angry (at Rolf getting his head stuck in the bin and trailing rubbish all over the kitchen floor, for example), she doesn't really look or sound angry, if you see what I mean. She just goes a bit tight-lipped and tuts a lot, usually. Secondly, she stopped talking when she saw me, like she was guilty or something. Wow – pre-wedding nerves must really have been getting to her. I hoped it wasn't poor Stanley at the other end of the line...

"Oh! Ally!" said Stanley in surprise, as I strolled into the kitchen and caught him sitting at the table, stuffing a letter or, more likely, a wedding invite into an envelope.

I was surprised to see him, since I'd thought my Grandma was currently giving him a piece of her mind on the phone, and he seemed just as surprised to see me, which was odd, considering I lived here and he didn't.

"Hi," I mumbled, flopping into the seat opposite him. "What's up with Grandma? She sounds a bit ... grouchy."

"What – on the phone just now?" Stanley asked me.

(A stupid question, really – what did he think I meant? That she was grouchy yesterday? Three weeks ago? Some time in 1972? Of *course* I meant now.)

"Yeah, on the phone," I nodded.

"Oh, don't worry about that," Stanley shook his balding, white-haired head kindly at me. "It's just an old friend of hers; she said she was coming to the wedding, and now she's not sure if she can make it and I think your gran's a little disappointed. But I suppose it's our own fault for deciding to go ahead with it at such short notice. It's like my sister Maisie; she's not sure if she can come because she had her holidays booked to the Isle of Wight and she doesn't know if she can change the dates because she's booked her dog in the kennels already and it's very hard to change kennel dates because of them being so booked up in the summer holidays and..."

When your head's full of weirdness, it's very hard to try and concentrate on stuff like Stanley's sister Maisie's problems with dog kennels, and even though I was trying *really* hard to look interested, I think sweet old Stanley could see that I patently *wasn't*.

"Oh, you know, I'm sure Rowan was looking for you, Ally," he told me, breaking off suddenly from the Maisie-and-her-boarding-kennel drama. "She popped down only a few minutes ago, asking if you were back yet. I think she's just upstairs in her room."

"Oh, right. Well, I'd better go and see what she wants!" I smiled, grateful to be allowed to zoom off.

And I did zoom – straight past Grandma, who was just putting the phone down, straight up the stairs past snoozing cats, and straight into Rowan's room without knocking.

"Ooh!" gasped Rowan, acting just as startled to see me as Grandma and Stanley had been. What was going on? Had I left the house looking like Ally Love and come back looking like a total stranger?

"What are you 'oohing' at?" I frowned, closing her bedroom door behind me.

"You surprised me – I'm making these, and I didn't want Grandma to see them yet!" she explained, holding up a home-made paper chain of a male and female figure holding hands. "It's supposed to be Grandma and Stanley – cute, isn't it?"

"Yeah, yeah. Anyway, do you want to know what happened round at the shop?" I asked her, settling myself down in her blow-up green chair.

(Out of nowhere, Colin the cat appeared and hopped on to my lap, instantly purring and padding.)

"Of course!" exclaimed Rowan, putting down her scissors and endless paper chain. "Tell, tell!"

"Well – *ow*!" I yelped, removing Colin's padding claws from my bare thighs before I carried on. "I'd only just started talking to Dad – all that round-about stuff you told me to start with – when Miss Woods walked in!"

"No!" Rowan gasped. "What did she want? What was she doing there?"

"She was taking a bike in for Dad to mend. He must have offered to do it when they were talking last night!"

I felt my heart physically deflating as I retold what had happened with Dad and Daisy Woods.

"So what else did they say? What did they talk about? Did they *twinkle*?" Rowan rushed her questions at me.

"Oh, *yes*, they *twinkled*," I told her, feeling my whole spirit sag. "But I don't know what else they said – I just made an excuse and left them to it."

"You *left*? Are you *mad*? You should have stayed and earwigged, Ally!" Rowan hissed at me.

Actually, it wasn't *her* that was hissing; and it wasn't just my heart that was deflating or my spirit that was sinking. After being gently pushed to one side (by me), Colin had continued to do his comfort clawing on the arm of the blow-up chair, and now that my bum was touching the carpet and I was leaning like the Tower of Pisa towards the arm of the rapidly flattening chair, it was obvious that I couldn't carry on this conversation sensibly.

And I didn't have to, 'cause right then Linn burst in (knocking as she threw the door open).

"Hi – what on earth are you doing, Ally?"

"Collapsing, like this thing," I mumbled, scrambling on to my knees as Rowan shooed Colin away to survey the damage to her precious chair (now a worthless pile of rubbery plastic).

"Well, Grandma says can you both come down, please," Linn announced, before turning and disappearing.

"What's she doing home?" I whispered to Rowan, as I struggled to my feet.

"She's only working a half day today," Rowan whispered back, her nose just a few centimetres from the plastic as she studied it for telltale claw puncture marks. "Do you think Dad could fix this with a puncture-repair kit from the shop?"

"Probably. Anyway, should we call Linn back? Tell her about Daisy and Dad?" I asked in hushed tones.

"No – not till we know more," Rowan instructed me, obviously thinking like I did that Linn wouldn't appreciate us jumping to conclusions like we did last time.

"OK," I agreed, though I wasn't sure if we were doing the right thing. "Well, come on then, let's see what Grandma wants..."

Pastel?!

"Thanks, Stanley, that's so sweet of you!" Linn was saying, ever the polite oldest sister (except to me and Ro, of course).

"It's my pleasure," Stanley was beaming happily. "There's nothing that would make me happier than treating you girls to new outfits for the wedding!"

Pastel?! my mind screamed, while Stanley talked.

"I just thought that what with it being an informal wedding," Grandma added, "it seemed to make more sense to let you girls wear what you want, since you all have very different styles."

"Thanks, Grandma!" smiled Linn. "I mean, I *would* have worn a bridesmaid's dress if you'd wanted us all to, but it's much nicer this way!"

OK, so Linn wasn't going to be forced out of her ever-present uniform of trousers and fitted tops and into a fluffy, flouncy bridesmaid's get-up, but was she actually *listening* to what Grandma had just said?

"Ooh, I can't *wait* to go shopping!" Rowan giggled, clapping her hands together.

Seemed like *she* wasn't listening either.

"Is that all right with you too, Ally, dear?" Grandma asked me, noticing my stunned silence.

"*Pastel?!*" I heard myself squeak out loud.

"Yes, you *know*; pastel, as in soft pink, peach, baby blue, mint green, lemon ... that sort of thing," Grandma replied, obviously assuming I was after an explanation, rather than squeaking through sheer horror. "It's just that I'll be wearing cream, and I'm going to have a bouquet of pastel roses, so it would be perfect."

Perfect for *Grandma*, maybe, but not for us bridesmaids. Amazingly, me, Rowan and Linn had one thing in common when it came to clothes – none of us would ever, ever willingly dress head-to-toe in *pastel*.

Omigod, we were going to look like the marshmallow sisters...

Chapter 11

KYRA AND THE HORRIBLE HOME TRUTHS

"Sorry."

"About what?" I asked Kyra. (I was taken aback – Kyra isn't the sort of girl to say sorry, *ever*.)

"About *them*. You were right; it *is* pretty *icky*…"

We both stared at one of the pedalos bobbing about on the duck pond (poshly called the "boating lake" by the powers-that-be who run the park at Alexandra Palace). The pedalo we were staring at happened to contain Sandie and Billy. They were out in the middle of the pond, close to the island packed with ducks and geese who looked thoroughly grouchy with all the people currently splashing around on row-boats and pedalos on *their* patch of water.

"I mean, why do they have to act so … dumb?" Kyra asked, her eyes glued to Billy (currently giggling and pretending to splash Sandie with water) and Sandie (currently giggling and pretending to be scared of Billy splashing her with water).

"'Cause they're all lovey-dovey. That's what you

told me. *You* said I had to expect this, 'cause that's the kind of stuff people in love *do*," I said, reminding her of the phone conversation we'd had on Sunday morning.

"Yeah, but I didn't think they'd be *this* drippy," Kyra grimaced, sticking her fingers in her throat and pretending to barf.

It was Thursday, and me, Kyra, Sandie and Billy were supposed to be having an afternoon hanging out together, but it seemed more like it was Billy and Sandie hanging out together, with me and Kyra tagging along uselessly in the background. Sandie and Billy had done nothing but whisper and snicker with each other since we'd all met up. You'd think the two of them had blinkers on, and couldn't even *see* us. I was quite tempted to go and stick my head between the two of them when they were gloopily gazing at one another, but the tetchy, touchy mood I was in, I couldn't be bothered. I was just glad that Kyra, at least, could see my point about the excess ickyness at last.

But that wasn't the *only* thing that Kyra could see.

"So..." she said, turning round on the bench and staring at me. "What's up with *you*?"

"What do you mean, what's up with me?" I asked her defensively.

"Come off it," she grinned. "You've been a total misery-guts. If you don't tell me what's wrong, I'll be forced to think that you're jealous of Sandie and secretly fancy Billy or something…"

"I do *not*!" I squeaked indignantly, startling a diddy little moorhen nearby and making it dart away from us *fast*.

"Well, what's the deal, then?" Kyra slouched back on the wooden bench. "'Cause you can't kid *me* – something's definitely up."

Telling your innermost secrets to Kyra Davies is about as sensible as stroking an alligator. But right then, I felt like blabbing my woes to the nearest person, and since Kyra was sitting about twenty centimetres away, she'd do.

"I think my dad might have a twinkle for someone."

"Excuse me? A *twinkle*?! Do you mind speaking *English*, please, Ally?" Kyra pulled a face at me.

"I think he might fancy someone," I reluctantly admitted out loud. "The same person Tor has a crush on."

"Your *dad* and your *brother* both fancy the same person? Urgh … that's *creepy*," shuddered Kyra, taking me too literally.

"It's not like *that*. It's Tor's teacher from his summer club thing," I tried to explain more clearly. "Tor's got a bit of a crush on her, but I think my dad might *really* like her."

"How come?" asked Kyra, stopping with the teasing and paying proper attention.

"He met her when we went to the circus two nights ago. And then she came to his shop yesterday when I was there. And then she went to his line-dancing class last night."

It was the business with the line-dancing class that was really getting me down. Miss Woods had still been in the shop – talking broken bikes and twinkling with my dad – when I left them yesterday afternoon, but it wasn't till he mentioned it at breakfast this morning that I realized he'd ended up asking her again to come along to his class that night – and she'd taken him up on it. I didn't care that she already knew someone who went there too; I just cared that Dad was smiling really widely this morning when he spoke about her. Which made Tor's face light up like someone had pressed a switch at the side of his head. Rowan, in the meantime, started choking on her cheese, peanut butter and jam toastie. Linn, I couldn't help but notice, went a bit pursed-lipped. Maybe it was time to talk to her about the dilemma of Dad and Daisy Woods…?

"What's she like, then, this teacher?" Kyra quizzed me.

"Well ... I dunno..." I faffed around, trying to think of words to describe Miss Woods. "Pretty ... not that old ... this mad, ringlety, red hair ... friendly ... a bit ditzy..."

"Sounds nice."

"Um, well, I guess she *is* nice."

"So, what's the problem? Your dad fancies someone new. So what?"

I *knew* I shouldn't have spoken to Kyra about this. I *knew* she wouldn't understand.

"But Kyra, how can he fancy someone new?"

"Well, what's to stop him?"

"How about my *mum*?" I stressed, raising my eyebrows at her.

"What *about* your mum? She's been gone four years, hasn't she? I think it's time your dad was allowed to have some fun," Kyra shrugged.

I couldn't talk for a second, I was so stunned.

"But ... but how can you say that?" I finally managed to splutter out. "My mum and dad are in love!"

"*Correction*," Kyra stared languorously at me. "They *were* in love. If your mum still loved your dad, she'd be here, not gadding about all over the world."

Ouch. Somehow, that felt *exactly* like she'd slapped me in the face.

"And while we're on the subject," Kyra continued, turning around in her seat to interrogate me. "Why doesn't she get in touch with you lot?"

"But she *does*!" I protested, feeling my cheeks – no, make that my entire *body* – flush lurid pink. "She sends letters and postcards and photos all the time! You've seen them on the board in the kitchen, and beside the map in my room! *And* she sometimes sends us little presents, too!"

"Yeah, but why does she always just post you stuff? Why can't she use a phone, like normal people? It's not as if she's stuck halfway up the Congo in a rainforest or something. She *does* go to countries with *cables* and *satellites* and stuff. So why can't she just call you now and again?"

Kyra looked so calm and cool and collected, like one of the presenters on those daytime talk shows, while I felt as if I was going to faint or maybe even self-combust. None of my other friends – not Sandie, not Billy, not Chloe or Salma or the others – had *ever* asked me anything like that. Whenever it came to the subject of my mum, everyone I knew was tactfully silent about it. And here was Kyra Davies, having the cheek to ask me something ... that I hadn't dared ask myself.

It was true. That was a question me and my

family never, *ever* asked out loud: why *didn't* Mum ever phone us?

"I mean, even when my mum was at her most horrible and maddest, she was still there for me to talk to," Kyra expanded, taking my silence as permission to prattle on. "Not that I *wanted* to talk to her most of the time, but you know what I mean."

I *did* know what she meant, but my head was too swirly to reply and all I could do was glance away towards the bobbing little moorhen on the pond and try and wait for my brain to unscramble.

"Hey, your mum – she really *is* away travelling around the world, isn't she?"

I flipped my head around towards Kyra's questioning face.

"Course she is! What are you on about?"

"Well, the travelling thing! It's not just a cover-up, is it? I mean, she's not in *prison*, is she?"

"*No!*" I hissed at her in shock. "God, Kyra! Are you nuts? Have you looked at any of the photos she's sent? Unless there are prisons on sunny beaches, then I think it's safe to say she *is* actually travelling! OK?!"

"OK," Kyra shrugged, unruffled by my defensive outburst.

"And anyway, what would my mum be in prison *for*? Being criminally nice?"

"She can't be *that* nice if she never bothers phoning—"

"Stop! Don't say anything else, Kyra!" I snapped, holding one hand up in front of her face. "You've never met her so you can't say *anything* about her!"

"Suit yourself," said Kyra casually, pulling a pack of chewing gum out of her pocket and offering me a piece.

I shook my head and stared off at the moorhen again, fizzing with rage at Kyra. Maybe she had a point about the phone call stuff (I'd have to give that serious thought when I was back in my room), but how *dare* she say horrible things about Mum?

"Hey, Ally! Check this out!" Kyra said suddenly, pointing towards the pond.

When I glanced over at the yellow pedalo, I was just in time to see Billy standing up, wobbling the boat from side to side while Sandie giggled and shrieked at him to stop. Sandie's shriek was immediately followed by a loud "*Oi!* Oi, *you!* Stop that NOW!" from the guy who rented out the boats. That shout seemed literally to catch Billy off-balance – right before my eyes he wobbled, then wibbled, then fell in slow-motion, splashing a tidal wave that sent all the ducks fluttering to safety as he landed slap-bang in the water.

Even though my head and heart were twisted in

knots, I couldn't help bursting out laughing, same as everyone else in the vicinity, as Billy – covered in silty, sludgy mud – struggled to his feet and started wading his soggy way out of the shallow water.

Ah well, Billy might have been a pretty lame friend in lots of ways at the moment, but at least the big berk could still cheer me up, even if he didn't *mean* to...

Chapter (12)

From now on, I decided, pastel would never be described as just "pastel". It would be described as "blee! pastel" at all times. (As in: "There's no way I'm wearing those – blee! – pastel trousers...")

It was Saturday afternoon. I had money (thank you, Stanley) burning a hole in my pocket. I had some serious shopping to do (i.e. finding something half-decent in – blee! – pastel to wear to Grandma and Stanley's wedding next weekend).

All I needed was a useful friend, or even a nutty sister (i.e. Rowan), to lend me a hand and give me a second opinion ("Ooh, banana yellow and mint green! That *really* suits you, Ally!"). But *did* I have a friend or nutty sister to help me out? No, I did *not*.

Rowan was hanging out with her goth mates Von and Chazza somewhere, Sandie was out with Billy (again), Kyra had gone somewhere with her parents (not that I was in the mood to see her for a couple of days, not after what she'd said about

Mum, even if bits of it were true), Chloe, Salma and Kellie were all doing family stuff too, and Jen was on holiday in Greece (what a feeble excuse!).

But all was not lost.

Someone with *impeccable* taste had taken time out to hang around in TopShop etc. with me today and give me the benefit of their intuitive fashion sense.

"What d'you think of these?" I asked, holding up a pair of baby-pink cotton trousers at arm's-length. "Would they be OK?"

My question was met by silence. The only sound came from the in-store music blasting from various speakers and some girls chatting and giggling over by the fitting room.

"Tor? *Tor?* What do you think?" I asked a little bit louder, spinning around to locate my little brother.

Still no reply. But some kind of animal instinct told me I should look for him at ground level...

"Aha!" I whispered to myself and smiled, as I spotted him curled up under a circular stand of sale-price boob-tubes.

Talking to himself again, I couldn't help but notice.

"Tor? What're you doing?" I asked, bending double to eyeball him.

"Nothing!" he said defensively, cutting out the

talking-to-himself thing, wriggling out from under the boob-tubes and scrambling to his feet. "Are you buying *them*? They're horrible!"

See? Tor might only be seven, but he still knew a thing or three about fashion.

"No," I shook my head, offloading the hideous baby pink trousers on to the nearest rail to me. "This is doing my head in. Fancy getting a doughnut and a juice?"

"Yeah!" Tor sighed happily.

"Come on, then!" I announced brightly, leading the way out.

I hoped I sounded as happy as Tor. I'd been trying *really* hard the last couple of days to seem happy, mainly because I'd lain awake on Thursday evening and decided that it was the best plan of action. After all, the most important thing coming up was Grandma and Stanley's wedding, and even after Kyra sending my head into orbit with mad thoughts about Mum ... well, I came to the conclusion that I should just try and shove those mad thoughts into a box in my head for the moment, and not go upsetting myself – and everyone else in my family – with all that stuff.

After all, talking about Mum wasn't going to change anything, was it...?

"So, are you looking forward to this thing we're all

going to tomorrow afternoon?" I smiled at Tor, as we strolled along the shopping centre concourse – hand-in-swinging-hand – heading towards the escalator.

"Yeah!" Tor nodded happily. "Do Dad's friends have pets?"

This was the main thing Tor wanted to know about the party we were all invited to. It wasn't anything fancy, or some wow-type do that I was all excited about – it was just a bit of a barbecue someone from Dad's line-dancing class was having in their garden in Crouch End, with everyone's families and kids invited along. I reckoned it would be kind of fun; as long as they didn't blast out (urgh) country music the whole time...

"I don't know if they've got pets, Tor. I don't think Dad knows either," I shrugged, as we took our place on the crowded up-escalator. "But if they've got a big garden, then hopefully it means they'd at least have a dog or a cat or something."

Tor nodded thoughtfully at what I'd just said, then stunned me by suddenly bolting as if he'd just been jabbed by a pointy stick. Next thing I knew he was diving up the escalator – past all the other shoppers – two at a time.

"Tor?" I called out after him, knowing I was too big to wend my way past everyone and their bags like he'd just done.

A few impatient seconds later, I arrived at the first floor concourse and gawped around, looking for my missing-in-action brother for the second time in five minutes.

A wave alerted me to his location. But not a wave from Tor – oh, no. The hand doing the waving was attached to an arm in a long-sleeved pink T-shirt with swirly Indian-style designs on it (Rowan would *kill* for that T-shirt), which in turn was attached to a person with a smiley, friendly face and wild, red, ringlety hair.

"Hi, Ally!" Daisy Woods called over to me, as Tor gazed up at her like she was Kylie Minogue and a chocolate fudge sundae rolled into one. "Lost someone?"

"Tor! Don't just run away from me like that!" I told him off gently, offering Daisy Woods a hint of a smile at the same time. "You'll give me a heart attack!"

"But I saw Miss Woods!" he protested.

Oh, and that made everything OK, did it? If the amazing Miss Woods was at the other side of a dual carriageway, with ten-tonne trucks thundering up and down at top speed, would Tor still go zooming over towards her? Probably...

"Tor, Ally's right! You should always let people know where you're going and not just run off and leave them!" Miss Woods said, raising her eyebrows at my bruv.

"OK…" Tor nodded at her earnestly.

Great – he was all set to go mumfy on me when *I* tried to tell him to be careful, but when it was Miss *Woods* doing the lecturing, he turned into the best boy scout.

"So Tor was just saying that you're off for dough-nuts?" Miss Woods turned and said chattily to me.

"Yeah, that's right – thought I'd treat him!" I smiled, grabbing Tor in what I hoped looked like a cute, sisterly bear-hug (I was actually trying to cover his mouth before he tried to invite Daisy along for a doughnut too).

"Well, I'm jealous. I'm off to buy some very boring pots and pans – and I better hurry because my car's on a parking meter," she said chattily, pushing her springy curls back off her face. I hadn't noticed she was so freckly before – not just across her nose, but over her whole face. Along with her v. cool, Rowan-style top, those all-over freckles made her look more like a girl than a grown-up teacher.

"Right…" I shrugged, not knowing what else to say.

Tor seemed to have something else to say, though – he'd grabbed my arm and was pulling my hand away from his mouth.

"Bye, Miss Woods!" he called out, as she started walking away. "See you tomorrow!"

Tomorrow? But tomorrow was Sunday. Tor didn't have one of his summer club craft class things tomorrow. He must have forgotten what day it was.

"Bye, Tor! Bye, Ally!" Daisy Woods beamed, in a haze of clashing pink T-shirt and red curls. "See you tomorrow!"

"Tor," I muttered through gritted teeth, as I smiled and waved at Miss Woods as she ambled off towards Pearson's department store, "what is she on about?"

"The barbecue!" said Tor, turning and frowning up at me as if I was acting the total muppet.

"The *barbecue*? You mean, the barbecue *we're* all going to tomorrow? Miss Woods has been invited to that *too*?" I checked with him, although I didn't exactly need to since it was now stupidly obvious to anyone with half a brain.

"It's *her* friend's house!" Tor carried on explaining. "But I forgot to ask her if they had pets!"

So ... once again, Daisy and Dad were going to meet.

Looked like me and Rowan were going to have to do some serious spying over our barbecue-burnt burgers...

Chapter 13

HUGE SURPRISE, NO. 2

When you're a bit unhappy or out of sorts, you're supposed to lose your appetite, right? Well, maybe that's true when you're at home and all there is to eat is some stale Rice Krispies and half a tin of week-old beans in the fridge. But when you're at a barbecue, faced with a trestle table that's absolutely *heaving* with gorgeous food, it's amazing how strong-willed your tummy gets, totally overruling your mind.

Now should I have ketchup on my burger? Or sweetcorn relish? Or salsa dip? Or all three...?

"Hey, how are you today, Ally?"

I was suddenly being asked this question by a looky-likey hound-thing, made out of a hot dog, with floppy "ears" (soggy bits of lettuce dangling from either side of the long bread roll), along with two eyes and a nose drawn on with squirty mustard. It was a piece of food sculpture that was worthy of Tor, but that dopey, cartoon voice didn't belong to my brother.

"Hi, there, little doggy!" I said to it enthusiastically, completely ignoring the person holding it. "Have you seen my friend Billy? He's kind of tall, skinny and stupid-looking..."

"Ha, ha, ha," grinned Billy, dropping the hot dog on to the table, and then thinking better of it and taking a massive bite out of it.

You know, I'd wondered if Billy would be here this afternoon – his mum and dad were fellow line-dancers along with Dad, and they would have been invited, I was sure. But I'd have thought that the only way they'd have got Billy here was to lasso him and drag him here kicking and screaming. But obviously I was wrong.

"So, wad 'appened do you dooday?" Billy mumbled through a mouthful of hotdog. "You dinnend durn up ad Awwy Pawwy dis monning."

"*Excuse* me?" I said, holding my hand to my ear. "I didn't quite catch that. Didn't your parents ever tell you that it's rude to talk with your mouth full?"

Hey, it wasn't the first time. Billy regularly tried to have phone conversations with me while he was hoovering who-knows-what into his gob. Well, as far as I *remembered*, that was the case. I hadn't had any phone conversations with him lately, so he might not have been guilty of doing that any more...

"I *said*," he began again, after gulping down his food, "what happened to you today? You didn't turn up at Ally Pally this morning."

Wow, I was quite surprised. I was sure Billy's brain was too fried with love to remember our regular dog-walking date (and don't go getting ideas when I use the word "date").

"I didn't think you'd be there, so I took Rolf and Winslet for a walk in Priory Park instead," I shrugged.

"Why didn't you think I'd be there?" Billy frowned under his baseball cap. "We *always* meet up in Ally Pally on Sunday mornings!"

"Yeah, but we always speak on the phone about three times a week, and you haven't returned any of my calls in the last fortnight," I pointed out.

Billy went a bit blushy, and started fidgeting with the brim off his cap.

"*And*," I continued, "the only times I've seen you is when you've been with Sandie! I've never *once* got to see you on your own!"

"Um ... well, here I am!" he joked, throwing his arms out wide.

I was going to tease him some more (he deserved to feel guilty for neglecting me, after all), but then I took one look at his goofy, grinning face and felt so chuffed to be hanging out with him – just me and him – that I couldn't be bothered. And any-way, the reason he'd come along with his mum and dad today was probably 'cause he knew I'd be here with Dad and my sisters and Tor. Yeah … this could be fun. We could catch up properly, have a laugh (and I could do with one of those), maybe fool around and have a contest to see who could eat a burger quickest. Or maybe I could dare him to eat spoonfuls of mustard and see how long it would take him to start sweating – it was really funny when he did that one time before with Worcester sauce. And then maybe—

"Hi, Ally! Isn't this a brilliant party?" Sandie bustled up and smiled, grabbing hold of my arm. "And have you seen inside the house properly? I just went to the loo upstairs and it has the most *huuuge*, old-fashioned, Victorian bath!"

My heart never, ever sinks at the sight of Sandie – not normally. But just this once, it catapulted right down to the grassy ground when my best friend appeared out of nowhere. Mainly 'cause that meant I wasn't going to get Billy to myself this once. *And* it meant I'd got it wrong; he hadn't come along to this barbecue today specially to see me – he'd come 'cause it was somewhere he could take Sandie.

Before I could regain my cool and answer

Sandie, someone *else* bustled up out of nowhere.

"Hello, Ally, dear!"

It was Billy's mum, looking as pristine and perfect as ever. I don't mean that as a compliment, by the way. It's just that she fascinates me, the way she always wears a tonne of immaculate make-up and smart, smart, smart clothes at all times, even when she's just hanging out at home, or at a barbecue or something. Like today, this whole garden was crowded with mums and dads and kids wearing jeans and T-shirts, or shorts and vest tops, or floaty cotton dresses (er, not the dads, of course). But Mrs Stevenson? She was wearing a navy *suit*, for goodness' sake, and these super-expensive looking (and super-*boring*-looking) navy and gold sandal things. And her face must have been melting under all that foundation and powder and lipstick. I mean, it was all very tasteful and elegant and everything, but it was just *so* uptight. How she and my mum got on so well in the past was totally weird, but they did. Maybe it was a case of opposites attract, even when it comes to friends.

But the fact that she had been friends with Mum – that was *another* reason that I was always a bit funny about Mrs Stevenson, *apart* from the fact that her hyper-neatness freaked me out. It was just that every time she saw me, she always had to ask (with head tilted sadly and sympathetically):

a) if we'd heard from Mum;
b) how we all were;
c) how our "poor father" was coping.

All of the above made me avoid talking to her whenever possible. (I tried to stick to stuff like, "Hello, Mrs Stevenson – yes, I'll have a biscuit, thank you. We're going up to Billy's room now. Bye, Mrs Stevenson!") But here she was, completely cornering me.

"Hi, Mrs Stevenson," I replied, warily.

(Out of the corner of my eye, I could see Sandie trying to hold Billy's hand and rest her head on his shoulder, and I could also see Billy step sideways away from her, grabbing a handful of peanuts from the table with the hand Sandie was reaching for, while her head bobbed awkwardly in mid-air. Clumsy boy...)

"So, Ally... I just wanted to ask – who's that pretty woman your dad's talking to? I saw her at line-dancing class this week, but I didn't get a chance to ask your dad who she was..."

I glanced over in the direction Billy's mum was noseying in, and spotted Dad – who'd been standing with Linn, Ro and Tor a few minutes ago – chatting (and, yes, *twinkling*) with Daisy Woods. Of course.

"It's Tor's summer club teacher," I explained, hoping I sounded casual enough (ha!). "Oh, sorry! Got to go – Linn is waving me over!"

Linn was doing nothing of the sort, but that white lie got me away from nosey Mrs Stevenson and the nauseatingly loved-up Billy and Sandie...

"...and I know we got it all wrong last time we thought Dad was seeing someone else, but *this* time – just the way they keep *twinkling* at each other – I think he might *really* start seeing Miss Woods!" I babbled to Linn, while Rowan nodded like a nodding dog toy beside me.

You know something? No matter how grouchy and unapproachable Linn could be, sometimes it felt great to offload everything to my big sister. Linn listened intently as I babbled on, without interrupting me or telling me that I was over-reacting or was going demented or something. Then she turned and stared across at Dad and Daisy, sitting chatting on the bench by the water feature. Me and Ro stared too, and watched as Tor – trailed by an adoring, elderly Labrador (the pet of the party-throwers) – shyly approached them, nudged Dad, handed him a tiny bunch of daisies, whispered in his ear, then ran away with the elderly Labrador bounding beside him like an arthritic puppy.

Dad and Daisy were both laughing, but Dad was looking kind of embarrassed too. Then he shrugged and handed the doll-size bouquet of flowers to a blushing Daisy, since that was obviously what Tor had whispered to him to do.

Good grief; what was Tor up to, acting like some kind of mini-matchmaker? He was only seven, for goodness' sake. Shouldn't he be over by the campfire with the other little kids, burning the roof of his mouth with toasted marshmallows, instead of doing this cupid routine?

"Dad already told me he likes Daisy," Linn said calmly. "I got in late last night, and ended up sitting talking to him for ages about all sorts of stuff, including her."

"You *knew*?" squeaked Rowan. "What did you say to him when he told you?"

"I told him I was pleased, if he thinks that he may have found someone he likes," Linn shrugged. "And then he went all shy on me, and told me not to go jumping to conclusions, 'cause he only said he *liked* Daisy."

"But Linn!" I panicked, knowing as well as she did that Dad even *mentioning* stuff like that *meant* something. "What about Mum?"

"Listen, Mum's been gone a long, long time now, and we don't know whether she's *ever* coming home. So, if there's a chance for Dad to meet someone else, someone who's really nice, why should any of us mind, really?"

"But how do you know she's nice?" Rowan jumped in, sounding alarmed. "I mean, I know this Miss Woods *seems* nice – right, Ally?"

I nodded. There was no arguing – Daisy Woods had definitely come across as undoubtedly nice the couple of times I'd met her.

"But how do we *know* she's really nice?" Ro continued.

"'Cause Tor really likes her, and he's always got good instincts about people, as well as animals, hasn't he?" Linn pointed out fairly to us.

Me and Ro said nothing – instead we just stared over at the chatting and twinkling going on between Dad and Daisy over by the water feature.

"And after I was talking to Dad last night, I just lay in bed thinking," Linn added. "I just thought, maybe we shouldn't be selfish. It's just that we all know what it's like to have a mum, but Tor doesn't, not really. He can't remember properly. So maybe, for his sake, if Dad and Daisy *did* hit it off…"

Linn didn't need to finish her sentence; me and Rowan got her drift. And no matter how tummy-flippingly, head-swirlingly, heart-tuggingly weird it was to think about, she had a point. OK, so it was early days (since Dad had only known Daisy for five minutes), but maybe Tor *did* deserve to have someone nice and mumsy (and not sisterly or grandmotherly) to give him cuddles. And maybe Dad deserved something along those lines too.

Good grief... What a huge surprise that I could even, in the *tiniest* way, begin to start to *possibly* get my head around that.

"Ally! I've been looking *everywhere* for you!" Sandie's traumatizing voice suddenly cut into me and my sisters' reverie.

"What's wrong, Sand?" I frowned, when I noticed the mega-drops of tears spilling down her cheeks and off the end of her nose.

"It's – it's – it's *Billy*!" she hiccuped unhappily. "He's been horrible to me. I-I-I-I want to go home!"

Now maybe Sandie's timing wasn't too hot since I was in the middle of a family crisis, and maybe she hadn't been the most excellent or attentive friend to me lately, but I certainly still had my brownie badge in Friendship Excellence and there was no way I was going to let my sobbing buddy wander home alone.

And *somewhere* amongst the jumble of thoughts and feelings clogging up my head, I couldn't help but make room for a *tiny* bit of curiosity about what had gone wrong between the lovey-doviest couple in Crouch End. (And no, I'm not talking about Grandma and Stanley, or even – eek! – Daisy and Dad…)

Chapter (14)

THE HUNT FOR – BLEE! – PASTEL

"*Yappitty-yappitty-yap-yap-yapp –*"

It was hard trying to concentrate on what Billy was saying, what with all the streamers and the barking.

"Watch, or you'll squash the doves, Ally!" said Rowan, as I nearly stepped back on to the flocks of white, pink and yellow paper birdies she had laid out along the whole length of the hallway, where she was stringing them together on lengths of sparkly silver wool in preparation for the reception at the weekend.

"Sorry," I mouthed back at her, tiptoeing my way round to the stairs, where I could carry on my phone conversation sitting safely tucked out of her way.

"*– itty-yappitty-yappitty-yap –*"

"*Shush, boy!* Aw, Ally, come on – you've *got* to help me!" Billy whined, while Precious – Billy's not-so-precious poodle – kept up a non-stop yapping in the background. "Sandie won't answer any of my calls! It's doing my head in!"

Join the club, mate, I thought darkly, remembering the last two weeks when the phone in our house had rung plenty of times, but it had never been Billy for me...

"– *pitty-yappitty-yappity-yappity-yap-yap-yappitty-yappi* –"

"But I've *tried*," I told him for the twelve trillionth time. "Sandie doesn't want to see you. Or talk to you. Or talk *about* you. In fact, she doesn't even want to talk to *me* if I happen to try and mention you. Hey, do you want to try and turn your dog down?"

It was Monday night, and all yesterday afternoon and evening, and now this evening too, Billy had been bombarding me, *begging* me to help him sort out the huge fall-out with Sandie, since she wouldn't speak to him on the phone. And she wasn't just blanking him *that* way; when he'd tried going round to her house to do some face-to-face grovelling, her mum had to sorrowfully tell him that Sandie didn't want to see him. At all.

"– *tty-yappitty-yappitty-yappity-yapp* –"

"But it's not fair, Al! *Shut up*, *Precious*. I mean, I really like Sandie – I just couldn't do it, not in front of my *parents*! Why doesn't she understand?"

Bad boy Billy. So what had he done that was so terrible?

Had he started flirting with another girl at the barbecue?

No.

Had he had a personality transplant and suddenly turned mean and obnoxious on Sandie?

No. (As long as you don't count talking with your mouth full of burger as being obnoxious.)

Had he eaten too many marshmallows, turned hyper with the sugar rush and done something rude, like try and put his hand up Sandie's T-shirt or something?

Nope – quite the opposite.

You want to know what his crime was? Well, brace yourself, you might be shocked... Through sheer mortification, Billy couldn't *quite* bring himself to be caught holding Sandie's hand in front of his parents – and Sandie took this as deep, *deep* rejection.

Now, I know Billy's a berk, but actually, I had to side with him over this one. To me, being spotted getting cuddly in front of your mum or dad would be as embarrassing as having my ultimate dream-boyfriend Alfie walk in on me having a wee or picking a spot in the bathroom mirror or whatever. But Sandie... Sandie just couldn't see it that way, no matter how much I tried explaining it to her when I attempted to calm her down on the walk home from the barbecue yesterday, or when we'd spoken since. "Ally, if he really, truly liked me, he wouldn't be ashamed of holding my hand – not in front of *anyone*!" she gulped tearily, over and over again. Honestly, there was no shaking her from the notion that she'd been hard done by.

"– *itty-yap-yap-yap-yappitty-yap-yappitty* –"

"What am I going to do, Al?" Billy asked plaintively.

"What – about your stupid dog, you mean?" I muttered, knowing, of *course*, that *wasn't* what he meant. "I'd get him a muzzle if I was you."

"No – not about *Precious*! About *Sandie*!" he replied, his lovelorn state making him too miserable to get my joke. "What if Sandie won't let me explain?"

You know, part of me felt sorry for Billy and Sandie – they both sounded so miserable. But another part of me wanted to knock their heads together and tell 'em to stop acting like a couple of muppets and sort it out. And then – please don't think I'm horrible – another part of me was kind of *glad* at the idea of them maybe splitting up. 'Cause that was the part of me that wanted everything back the way it used to be, when I was lucky enough to have two brilliant friends who liked to spend time with me, instead of forgetting I existed…

"Maybe you should try writing her a letter, tell her how you feel *that* way," I advised him.

"– *yap-yap-yappitty… Grrrrrrrrrrrrrrrrrrrrrr!*"

"Precious! Leave that plant alone! Mum'll go mad!"

"Billy, are you listening to me?"

"Yeah, yeah. But a *letter*? Like writing and envelopes and stamps and stuff?" snorted Billy, as if I'd just suggested something totally medieval. "Couldn't I just send her an e-mail?"

"*Yeah,*" I nodded, though he couldn't see me. "You *could* just send her an e-mail. And she *could* just delete it, as soon as she sees who it's from!"

Boys … they don't *get* romance, do they? I mean, yeah, it's nice to get an e-mail or a text message (at least I imagine it *would* be – I just don't happen to have a mobile or a computer at home). But a card or a letter … that's something special, isn't it? That's something you keep and you treasure. Even if Sandie was still mad at Billy, I couldn't see her chucking away a letter that Billy had taken the time and trouble to write and post. (Unless of course his imagination only got as far as writing something lame like, "Hi Sandie. Really soz. Billy xxx". And I wouldn't put it past him.)

Anyway, I didn't get a chance to say any of that, because She-Who-Must-Be-Obeyed (Linn, on her day off from her holiday job) was now standing beside me, shoving her wrist – and her watch – in my face.

"Billy, I've got to go. Linn is very subtly hinting that we're going to be late meeting Grandma."

"*Grrrrrrrrrrrrrrrrrrr-rowff!!*"

"*Precious!* Put that rubber tree down! *NOW!*"

"Bye, Billy!"

"No – hold on! Come on, Ally, you see your gran all the time! Can't you stay and talk to me some more?" Billy pleaded with me. "It's an emergency!"

"And so's this," I informed him. "There's six days till the wedding and we've got nothing to wear."

Oh, yes. The Love girls were going out en masse, to buy – blee! – pastel somethings for the wedding.

Wish us luck...

Me, Linn and Rowan – we'd been stood up. By our grandmother, of all people.

She'd got caught up in last-minute wedding arrangements apparently. Which is why the three of us ended up in Dorothy Perkins, shopping for our bridesmaids' outfits with a bemused and apologetic Stanley, who Grandma had sent in her place.

"Ooh, that's *lovely* on you!" cooed the shop assistant in charge of manning the fitting rooms.

Compliment or not, Linn looked like she might cry. Either that or she was going to grab the multi-coloured "1" garment, "2" garment, "3" garment plastic tokens the shop assistant was holding and ram them down her throat.

"Um ... give us a twirl, then!" Stanley asked in a warily cheerful voice.

Ever so reluctantly, Linn twirled (OK, make that *shuffled*) around, giving me, Rowan and Stanley a 360° view of the long, sleeveless, linen dress she was wearing. It was very grown-up and smart. And Linn likes smart. But Linn doesn't a) wear dresses (the last time I saw her in one was at the school charity fashion show last Christmas – but that *was* for charity), or b) wear – blee! – pastel. Linn's entire wardrobe consists of black, grey, black, white and some more black. I don't mean *goth* black (not like Rowan's mates Chazza and Von) – I mean smart, neat and trendy black. Boot-cut trousers, tight fitted tops, fitted jackets; that's the sort of thing Linn's into. Floaty, girly-pink dresses ... well, it didn't matter how plain this dress was, it was about as "Linn"-ish as me wearing red, patent hotpants and six-inch strappy stilettos.

And poor Linn – she wasn't the only Love sister hyperventilating in a panic. Rowan had managed to spot a flouncy gypsy top in baby blue that was semi-decent, but she was being driven half-*mad* by lusting over tons of gorgeous but non – blee! – pastel-coloured clothes in every shop we'd gone into. And me? Well, I was just going into denial and hoping Grandma would have a change of heart and drop the whole – blee! – pastel thing. (I wish...)

"Honestly, Linn, that ... that looks super-dooper on you!" poor Stanley blustered, holding one thumb aloft. "You look ... top of the pops! Definitely!"

I could see Rowan shooting me a sideways look, but I didn't dare catch her eye, in case I started sniggering at poor old Stanley's attempt at teen-speak. And anyway, Linn looked super-dooper unconvinced, and very wobbly around the edges, if you asked me.

"Yeah!" Rowan tried to join in, obviously deciding now that she should try and back up Stanley's super-dooper, top-of-the-pops comments. "That dress makes you look ... all peachy, Linnhe!"

Peachy.

Linnhe.

Wow – Linn was *really* going to love being described as "peachy", not to mention having her much-hated full name used in front of witnesses. I know Rowan was trying to be nice but she should have just kept her mouth shut.

"Ally? *You'll* tell me the truth, won't you?" Linn stared hard at me, her pretty face contorted as if someone was pulling out her toenails with tweezers.

"It's a nice dress," I said honestly. "Maybe on someone else, though…"

I hadn't meant to say that last bit – it just slipped out. But immediately, Linn went white and started reaching for the zip at her back, even though she was standing outside the fitting rooms in the main shop floor.

Luckily, that's when sweet, bumbling, out-of-his-depth Stanley said *exactly* the right thing.

"OK! Stuff the shopping! We're all going to eat cake!"

Bless him. Stanley had a couple of grown-up sons (that we'd never met) and some practically grown-up grandsons (that we'd also never met), but he'd had no personal, one-to-one experience with teenage girls, so super-dooper, top-of-the-pops points to him for gauging the mood *just* right and taking us all for a mega cake-eating experience in the café in the shopping centre *just* as things were about to go horribly wrong…

"Nice, is it, Linn?" Stanley beamed, as Linn tucked happily into her nearly devoured cheesecake.

Linn nodded happily, as she stopped to brush a

stray crumb off the long sleeve of her zip-up black top.

"Oooh, there's nothing like a nice chocolate eclair," Stanley sighed, contentedly patting his round tummy, after beating us three to it and scoffing all of his cake already.

"Is that your favourite, then?" I asked him, just before I took another bite of my strawberry tart.

"Oh, yes!" He nodded his white-edged bald head emphatically. "I was trying to persuade your gran to have a giant chocolate eclair instead of a wedding cake, but she's just not having it!"

This was quite fun. We'd got used to having Stanley around the past few months, but today we were finding out loads of stuff we never knew about him. Apart from his addiction to chocolate eclairs, we'd found out that his favourite colour was orange ("Reminds me of sunsets I've seen on holiday!"); that he once rode a camel on a trip to Egypt ("They have *shockingly* bad breath, you know!"); and that his 18-year-old grandson Jamie had dreadlocks and was secretly dating a divorced mum of two who was ten years older than him ("His mum and dad are terribly old-fashioned and stuffy! He knows they won't approve, so that's why he's only told me!"). I didn't know about my sisters, but what he'd told us made me *ache* to go on holiday abroad (which I'd never done), to see the Pyramids and get close enough to a camel and see how smelly its breath really was. That wasn't going to happen in a hurry, but at least we'd get to meet wild-child Jamie and the rest of Stanley's family on Saturday.

"Hey, speaking about the wedding cake," said Rowan, picking up the last few crumbs of blueberry muffin from her plate with her finger, "did you know that Tor's making little painted clay figures to go on the top of it? They're supposed to be of you and Grandma!"

"Rowan! You shouldn't have said!" Linn frowned at her. "I think Tor wanted it to be a surprise!"

"Not to worry. It's probably just as well to know they're supposed to be us – just in case we offend him by not recognizing ourselves!" Stanley smiled at both my sisters. "So is he busy making these works of art at his craft class today?"

"Uh-uh," Rowan nodded.

"Well, *that's* good. If his teacher is helping him, there's more of a chance of them looking like me and your gran, and not small woodland creatures or something!"

Stanley was only fooling around, making gentle fun of Tor's animal obsession. I guess he was supposing that we would all find that funny, but only Linn grinned – me and Rowan were still feeling mighty strange about the whole concept of Miss Woods in general. Not only were we reeling from shock that Linn was so accepting of Daisy and Dad getting matey, but something else had stumped us too: that business with Tor speaking to himself all the time? Well, Daisy had discovered his little secret, as she explained to Dad yesterday at the barbecue. She'd spotted him doing it in class – yakking to thin air as he made a papier mâché hippopotamus – and asked what was going on. Turned out Tor thought it would be fun to have an imaginary friend, and visualized himself a mate called "Troy", of all things.

The whole notion of Tor dreaming himself up an imaginary friend was odd (not as odd as calling him "Troy" though), and I hoped he hadn't done it because he was feeling lonely or anything. But what particularly felt odd was that Tor had decided to spill his secret to Daisy Woods, and not one of us...

"Don't mind them!" Linn laughed, nodding her head at me and Rowan after she copped the puzzled expression of Stanley's face at our lack of smiles. "They're finding it hard to get their heads around the fact that Dad might actually fancy someone!"

"*Sorry?* What – *what* did you say?" Stanley suddenly burbled in confusion. "Your dad has a *fancy* for someone?"

It sounded quite funny, a guy of Stanley's age using the word "fancy", even if he didn't exactly use it in the right way.

"Yeah ... we think Dad quite likes Tor's teacher," Linn shrugged, "and she likes him back, we're pretty sure."

"Oh..." mumbled Stanley, frowning till his hairy, white eyebrows banged together.

And – whoosh! – instantly my allegiances changed. *Stanley* had found love second time round, with our gran, so what gave him the right to look so disapproving at the news that Dad might have found someone else? Like Linn said on Sunday, didn't Dad deserve to be happy too?

As soon as that thought had popped into my mind, I realized I was now a whole 50% sure I could live with Daisy and Dad being together after all.

Well, if you gave me enough time to get my dumb, worrisome head around it...

Chapter 15

FRISBEES, FUN AND FROLICS (YEAH, *RIGHT...*)

It's lucky that I can trust my dogs. Right now, all I could see of them were two hairy dots in the green, grassy distance, as they played madly with an elderly Alsatian and a hyperactive Jack Russell that they were both old friends with.

Speaking of friends...

"Lemme see..." said Kyra, with her usual non-existent charm, grabbing the seashell choker out of Chloe's hand.

"It's really pretty, Ally!" Kellie said admiringly, as she watched the choker changing hands.

"I'd love something like that – it would go with my tan!" sighed Jen, pointing out her newly golden skin for the millionth time since we'd all met up.

Jen had just got back from her holidays in the early hours of the morning, but she was so desperate to catch up with us all that she'd come along to the park this Tuesday afternoon, even though she should probably have been catching up with her snoozles at home. We were all here in the park at Ally Pally because Chloe had come up with the ace idea of an unofficial sports day, to cheer us all up since the holidays were nearly over and we'd all be back at school next week. The "sports" were going to consist of rounders, Frisbee chucking, and an egg and spoon race. (Chloe had nicked a box of half-a-dozen free-range eggs from her dad's shop.) But it was an "unofficial" sports day, because it was going to include lots of lazing about gossiping and eating, and we had a strict rule that we hadn't to take any of the sport stuff seriously. (In fact, anyone being competitive would be severely frowned upon. Extreme silliness was the whole point.)

So here we all were – me, Chloe, Kellie, Salma, a suntanned Jen and Kyra – waiting (im)patiently for Sandie to turn up so the silliness could start. In the meantime, I was taking the opportunity to show off the really cool present that had arrived in the post that morning.

"What's it made of?" asked Kyra, squinting at the weirdly coloured flat shell dangling on the simple strip of fine, sand-coloured leather. In some lights, it seemed pearly white, and then it'd turn silvery piny-blue, next time you looked.

"It's mother-of-pearl," I explained. "It said so on the little velvet bag it came in."

"S'nice..." Kyra nodded.

"I know. Mum's got good taste."

I got a kick out of saying that to Kyra, after she'd bad-mouthed Mum when we were hanging out together last Thursday at the duck pond. So much for Mum not caring about us – what uncaring mother would send her three daughters the most gorgeous matching pendants, out of the blue? We were all so chuffed when they arrived this morning. Mum couldn't have known, but they were perfect for the wedding – even if me and my sisters didn't have any clothes to wear for it yet.

"Yooo-*hooooo*!"

"Look!" Kellie exclaimed. "Here comes Sandie at last!"

"Oh, God…" growled Kyra. "*Please* tell me she hasn't got a *baby* in there."

"Well, Kyra, I don't suppose she's just using that buggy to push a bag of nachos around here…" I told her, as I waved and watched Sandie veer off the path and rumble the buggy across the uneven grass.

"Oooh, how cute! We get to meet Sandie's little sister at last!" Kellie beamed, running over for first peeks, followed closely by Jen.

"Yeah, yeah – *very* cute. But how are we supposed to play games and muck around with a baby to look after?" I heard Chloe mumble darkly to Salma.

Uh-oh – while Kellie and Jen seemed charmed at the idea of meeting Miss Walker Jnr, Salma, Chloe and Kyra were less than thrilled, obviously seeing it more as a babysitting hindrance than a baby-bouncing treat.

Me? Well, I'd seen Bobbie a few times already, and fun as it was to coo for a while at the teeny-tinyness of her, it has to be said that really *weeny* babies get kind of *boring* after a while. It's just that you can't do much with them. At least bigger, fatter, older babies laugh like drains when you do peek-a-boo or tickle their tummies or blow raspberries at them. But really *weeny* babies ... well, basically they just sleep, cry, eat and poo, no matter how cute they look.

"Hi, everyone!" Sandie smiled, as she negotiated the buggy in our direction.

"Hi, Sand!" I replied, along with everyone else. "So how come your mum let you take her out today?"

I asked this while even our most reluctant friends did The Right Thing and peered in at the sleeping baby Bobbie. And I asked this because curiosity was killing me: the idea of Sandie's mum treating her as responsible enough to look after her sister alone was pretty stunning. But Sandie soon set me straight; it wasn't that her mum trusted her

– Sandie had ended up as chief nanny today due to desperation.

"Dad's away at a conference in Glasgow, and Bobbie cried the whole night," Sandie explained, stepping away from the buggy to give everyone else a chance to gawp inside. "Mum got no sleep at all – so she asked me to take Bobbie out for a couple of hours, or else."

"Or else what?" I asked.

"Or else she was going to go off her head," Sandie shrugged. "Plus she gave me this…"

Sandie took out a white piece of paper from her jean-skirt pocket, and began reading.

"*If Roberta wakes up from her nap and starts crying, then blah-blah-blah,*" Sandie droned, impersonating her mum's ever-so-slightly patronizing tone. "*If she doesn't want that, then try blah-blah-blah, or blah-blah-blah. If that doesn't work, then come straight home. Don't let her play with other babies, or put her down on the grass in case she gets germs. Make sure you keep her warm; but not too warm, because blah-blah-blah. If she is too warm then blah-blah-blah, or if she's too cold, then her fleecy blanket is packed away under the blah-blah-blah. If you have any doubts, then call me blah-blah-blah…*"

The "blah-blah-blah"s – Sandie wasn't actually

saying them, it's just that I was tuning out. Not because it was boring (which it was, incidentally), but because I was distracted 'cause I was watching Billy walking towards us, hands in his pockets, looking self-conscious. Good grief – this was *my* fault. When he'd phoned my house earlier, I'd told him that I couldn't talk, 'cause I was just on my way to meet all the girls at Ally Pally. It hadn't clicked in my stupid head that he'd snaffle that piece of information and see this afternoon as his perfect opportunity to approach Sandie.

Urgh...

"Um, Sandie ... can I talk to you for a sec?" he asked, surprising her as she was reading out the never-ending list of baby-rules she'd been given.

"Billy!" she squeaked in alarm. "I *don't* want to talk to you!"

"But Sandie, please!" Billy begged, stepping towards her and pushing his baseball cap back off his forehead to reveal a traumatized, pale face.

"Billy, maybe you should—" I tried to intervene, but before I could get any further, a protective wall of girlies had appeared – as if by magic – between him and Sandie.

"Hey, didn't you hear what she said? She doesn't want to talk to you!" said Jen, who might have only been back in the country five seconds but still seemed to be up to speed with all the latest happenings in Sandie and Billy's (non-existent) love-life.

"But I—" Billy started to protest, faced with a defence line-up of Chloe, Jen, Kellie and Salma. (Kyra was over by baby Bobbie, trying to soothe the cries now whining their way out of the buggy by putting her finger to her mouth in a desperate *shushing* action. Didn't Kyra know that two-and-a-bit-week-old babies can hardly even focus on a finger held two centimetres from their nose?)

"You *heard*," Chloe snarled at Billy, as Sandie cowered behind her. "Bog off!"

It was the combination of the two things really; someone telling poor, bemused Billy to bog off, and Sandie cowering like he was an axe-wielding maniac, and not just a boy in love, trying to make things right. Good grief, *someone* had to be on Billy's side.

"Look, stop giving him a hard time!" I heard myself jump in. "He's only trying to—"

"*Excuse* me?!" Chloe asked me, in that occasionally alarming stern tone that she can do so well. "Whose side are you on, Al?"

"I'm not on anybody's side!" I tried to protest, feeling everyone's eyes on me. "I'm just trying to say—"

But I didn't get a chance to say what I wanted to say because baby Bobbie's snuffly cries suddenly escalated to car-alarm volume (so much for Kyra shushing her). And Winslet and Rolf had appeared out of nowhere, with Winslet sneakily making off with our Frisbee while Rolf was barking himself into a frantic doggy frenzy at the sight of park ranger driving his put-putting buggy across the grass.

"Bobbie, I'm coming!" Sandie yelped.

"Sandie!" Billy yelped.

"Get lost, Billy!" Chloe yelped.

"*Rrrrruuuffffff!*" Rolf yelped.

You know something? All of a sudden I found myself wishing it was next week and we were all back at school already. Yep, compared to this, I was pining for the normality and tranquillity of a dull, boring old maths lesson.

And as you know, you'll never hear me say *that* too often...

Chapter 16

WOBBLY HEARTS AND STICKY DOVES

"Rowan, what will we do now?"

"Cut out hearts!" Rowan ordered Tor (and Sandie), handing them more sheets of thick pink paper. "We've got plenty of doves and cupids, but we need *lots* more hearts!"

It was Wednesday and with three days to go to the wedding, Rowan was acting like a woman possessed, whirling through the house, trailing decorations and brandishing scissors and glue wherever she went.

Sandie had picked the wrong morning to come round for tea and sympathy from me; no sooner had her bum touched the chair in the living room, than Rowan had roped her in as an extra pair of hands, since me and Tor weren't working fast enough for her liking.

And I wasn't working at *all* right that second – I was answering the phone to Kyra.

"Hiya-*aaaaaaaaah!*" she yawned at me, as though it was 7.30 a.m. and not quarter-past eleven in the morning. "What are you up to?"

"Making decorations for the wedding," I replied, as I watched a cat that wasn't Colin try and shake loose a dove that had somehow got glued to its paw. (A *paper* dove, that is, not a *real* one. I think it would be very difficult for a real live dove to become accidentally glued to a cat's foot. But you never know.)

"Has Rowan got you doing that, then?" Kyra lazily enquired.

"Yeah, me and Tor – and Sandie's here too, helping out."

As I spoke, I leant forward a little and peered into the living room. I could see Sandie staring mournfully and meaningfully at the wobbly-edged heart she'd just cut out.

Oh dear…

"Sandie? Is she still all mopey over Billy, then?" asked Kyra, sounding a little perkier now that she had something to gossip about.

"Yep."

(I couldn't say much more than "yep", not with Sandie sitting within earwigging distance. Although she was so wrapped up in her mopey thoughts that she probably hadn't even noticed I'd left the room yet.)

"Well, if she's still all mopey, then it means she's still mad about him," Kyra pointed out. "So why doesn't she just forgive the big, gangly git and go back out with him?"

"Don't ask *me*," I shrugged.

Dating ... it seemed like you had to be either giddily happy going out with someone, or gloomily miserable. Wasn't it possible to meet somewhere in the middle? Like be boringly happy together? Or even just quite OK? That would do for me; going out with someone nice, being boringly happy and feeling quite OK. But maybe that's not allowed when you're in love. And let's face it, what do I know about being in love anyway?

"I felt *so* sorry for Billy yesterday in the park; him slinking away 'cause of Chloe and all of them giving him a hard time."

"I know," I agreed with Kyra, remembering how I spotted a wistful look on Sandie's face as he slouched off, baseball cap pointing forlornly at the ground. I'd been sure she was going to give in and run after him, forgiving him for his bad handling of the public hand-holding situation. But she didn't – mainly, I think 'cause she was too scared of what Chloe and everyone would think since they'd just stood up for her so staunchly. I mean, *I* was pretty jumpy after them giving me a hard time for sticking up for Billy. We all made up though (not counting poor Billy), after taking turns trying to calm down screaming baby Bobbie and then being so stressed out and tired that we spent the afternoon doing nothing more strenuous than sunbathing and stuffing our faces. (We wouldn't have been able to play Frisbee anyway, since Winslet growled at anyone trying to take it off her.)

"So ... got your outfit for the wedding yet?" asked Kyra, changing the subject.

"Er, no," I mumbled, realizing that Grandma would be round later today sometime and would *not* be too thrilled to find that I – like my sisters – still had nothing to wear.

"What?!" squeaked Kyra. "Good grief, Ally! Right – that's it. Me and you are going to go into the West End this afternoon and do some serious shopping!"

"Um ... *OK*..." I agreed warily, knowing that it's virtually impossible to say no to Kyra Davies.

"There's only one thing..."

"What?"

"*Please* say Sandie can't come. I don't mean to be mean, Ally, but I couldn't stand a whole afternoon of her moping. I think I liked it better when her and Billy were being all lovey-dovey and icky!"

"S'all right," I dropped my voice to a tiny whisper, "she's got to be home by one 'cause her auntie's visiting."

I didn't mean to be mean either, but I knew exactly what Kyra meant. Specially since right this second, I could see Sandie sighing soulfully and tearing her wobbly, cut-out heart in half...

"Promise me something, Ally," said Kyra, as she stared into the tiny mirror and tried to apply the new sparkly lilac eyeshadow she'd just bought. (Very hard to do when you're on the top of a bus trundling up Crouch Hill.)

"Promise you what?" I asked, staring warily at the plastic bags at my feet. The stuff she'd twisted my arm to buy? Well, the *style* of the clothes was all right. But the colours? Let's just say I'd never be able to look at myself in the wedding photos...

"Promise me that if I ever go moony over a boy like Sandie has, can you just shoot me?"

"I promise," I nodded, thinking that there were plenty of times that Kyra was so annoying in general that I'd be very pleased to have an excuse to shoot her.

"Anyway, I've decided that I'm definitely off boys," she prattled on, still struggling to smear her eyeshadow in the right places (i.e. her eyelids and not her cheeks or nose) as the bus rumbled and raced along. "They're all a waste of time. Look at Ricardo, and Sam..."

Yuck – I'd rather not. Kyra had a habit of snogging good-looking but particularly obnoxious lads, the sort I'd rather not clog up valuable brain space thinking about, thank you very much.

"...but then there is this really cute boy doing a paper round in our street just now. Last Sunday morning he was *definitely* eyeing me up."

Aha – I knew the Queen of Flirt wouldn't be able to stick to her no-boy resolution for more than five minutes.

"What do you think, Ally?"

At first, I thought she was asking my opinion on whether or not the paper boy was head-over-heels in lust with her. But she didn't mean that at all – she was batting her eyes furiously, showing off her new, only slightly smudged eyeshadow.

As I struggled to think of a suitable compliment ("Yeah ... very spangly"), my attention was caught by something out of the bus window. It wasn't the panoramic view you get of Alexandra Palace as you get to the top of Crouch Hill – it was the sight of my Grandma and Stanley coming out of a local hotel, holding hands with a small girl in a pink sun-hat.

What was *that* all about...?

Chapter 17

PARANOIA AND SNAIL PATROL

Thursday, 5.45 p.m. Exactly forty-two and a quarter hours till Grandma and Stanley's wedding.

"Hmm…" I hmmed darkly, staring at the stuff I'd just tipped out of the plastic bags and chucked on Rowan's bed.

"Hmm…" Rowan hmmed dubiously, as she laid out the pale blue gypsy top she'd already bought, plus a long, white, layered petticoat skirt.

"What are you two 'hmming' about?" asked Linn, suddenly stopping outside Rowan's open bedroom door.

"We're not sure about the things we're wearing to the wedding," I turned and told her.

"Me neither," groaned Linn, coming into the room and pulling something out of the posh thick paper bag that had the name of the shop she worked in stamped on it. "I got these on staff discount today 'cause I was desperate. And don't ask me *what* shoes I'm going to wear…"

And so Linn's newly bought smart matching

jacket and trousers landed on the bed beside me and Rowan's "bridesmaid" outfits.

"You know, it's such a pity, but there was such a *gorgeous* burgundy version of this in the shop!" Rowan sighed, fingering her wishy-washy, pale blue top.

"I mean, it's all nice stuff and everything," Linn shrugged, surveying our haul. "But ... I don't know ... it just doesn't ... I mean, they just don't...

"...really go together!" I moaned.

It was true. The top I'd ended up with was a baby pink, long-sleeved T-shirt, with a big, pink sheeny-shiny rose motif on the front. My trousers were cream, baggy cotton ones, with a bit of delicate pink and green embroidery around the bottom, and around the pockets. Rowan had her blue floaty top and white Victoriana skirt, and Linn's suit was a soft, powdery lilac. All lovely (on other people), but they just didn't seem to work together. None of us had wanted to wear uniform bridesmaids' dresses (and thank goodness Grandma hadn't wanted us to) but this all looked like a big – blee! – pastel disaster. The only thing that would be matching was the mother-of-pearl chokers we'd all be wearing...

"Wait! I've got an idea!" Rowan exclaimed, her eyes lighting up in that worrying way of hers.

"What?" Linn frowned at her.

"Not going to tell you in case it doesn't work," Rowan announced, stepping hurriedly into her sparkly Indian mules. "S'cuse me – got to get to Woolworths before they close, *and* I've got to go to a few newsagents' shops…"

And with that, she flip-flapped her way out of the room at high speed, leaving me and Linn staring at each other, wondering what on earth was rattling around in that mystery of a mind of hers…

Paranoid.

That's what I was. Or at least, that's what I'd been like recently. Maybe it was the stress of the wedding rubbing off on me. I mean, I'd got myself in a tizz about Billy and Sandie getting together and forgetting about me, and now I was feeling sorry for them being split up. Then I'd got in a tizz about Daisy and Dad, and really, nothing much had happened between them so far, had it? They were hardly announcing their *engagement* or anything. They hadn't even been on a *date* yet. And like Linn said, so what if that did happen? (Um… I think I was still only 50% used to that idea.) *Then* I'd got myself in a really *dumb* tizz just now about our wedding outfits. And who really cared if me and my sisters looked like three uncoordinated marshmallows for one day, as long as it made Grandma happy?

"Staying for tea, Stanley?" asked Dad, walking into the kitchen, rubbing at his newly showered wet head with one of our pink towels.

"No, no – my sister and her family are here for the wedding, so I'm off out with them," Stanley replied, as he stood up from the kitchen table.

Duh! Of course! Yet *another* thing I'd got in a tizz about! I'd forgotten I'd spotted Grandma and Stanley yesterday outside that hotel in Crouch End with the little girl in the sunhat – but now it made sense! All of Stanley's friends and family would be starting to arrive in advance of the wedding! So that explained that. But I wasn't sure what the explanation was for the yelling going out in the garden just now...

"Nooooooooooooooo!"

Tor's yelp nearly made me, Linn, Dad and Stanley jump out of our skins. Had he hurt himself? Had one of the pets hurt themselves? Had his imaginary friend Troy fallen off the swing and bumped his imaginary head?

"What's up?" asked Dad, as we all rushed outside to see what the matter was.

"She wants to *kill* them!" Tor shrieked, pointing to Grandma, who was holding a plastic carton in her hand, looking like she was just about to tip the contents out over the big terracotta pots she'd spent the afternoon stuffing full of fat, raspberry-ripple-coloured flowers.

"Why do you want to do that, Irene?" asked Dad, bemused. "Didn't you just get those flowers today?"

"Not the *begonias*!" Grandma sighed irritably. "I'm putting some ... *stuff* down to ki— *stop* the snails and slugs eating the plants!"

"It's *poison*!" roared Tor dramatically. "She's going to *kill* them!"

"But Tor, Grandma just wants the plants to look nice for the wedding reception on Saturday," Dad tried to reason, now he understood what was going on. "You can't have lots of lovely flowers with big bites out of them on such a special occasion!"

"But *I* can make them stop!" Tor announced earnestly.

"How?" asked Linn.

"I can... I can do Snail Patrol! With a bucket! I'll collect them all!"

"And *then* what?" asked Linn, her hands on her hips.

"Me and Ally – we can take them to the park an' set them free!!"

Everyone stared at Tor, then turned grinning to

me. Great – I was now going to be a snail minder, escorting Tor and his bucket of slithery things round to Ally Pally.

Oh, well, anything for a peaceful life…

"Fine," I shrugged.

"Well, that's that sorted," said Grandma, matter-of-factly, screwing the cap back on the snail-killing carton. "Oh, and while I remember, Stanley and I wanted to say, please all feel free to ask your friends to the wedding reception. I know we're not having too many people at the ceremony, but we'd both like it to be open house here on Saturday – especially since it is *your* house!"

"Thanks, Grandma!" smiled Linn. "I'll go and phone Alfie, and Mary and Nadia too!"

Thanks, Grandma! I thought, feeling warm inside at the mention of Alfie's name…

"And it would be lovely to see Billy and Sandie … and that Kyra girl too," Grandma said to me.

Eek! Sandie and Billy in the same vicinity? I wasn't sure how *that* was going to work…

"Can I bring a friend too, Grandma?" asked Tor, cheering up now that he'd won a reprieve on the lives of the resident snails and slugs.

"Of course, Tor! Who do you want to come along? Freddie? Or—?

"Troy!" Tor announced.

I tell you, there was a lot of lip-biting going on in our garden – everyone knew how seriously Tor could take things and no one wanted to laugh out loud at his imaginary buddy.

"We'd *love* it if Troy came," said Stanley, patting Tor warmly on the shoulder.

"And Miss Woods, too?" Tor smiled innocently up at Stanley and Grandma.

"We'll see!" Dad laughed, bending down and picking up the first of many snails for Tor's collection. "I'm planning on asking a few of my friends from line-dancing class to come along, and I guess Daisy counts as one of those now!"

Aha, I thought, sneaking a sideways glance at Linn. *Surely that means Daisy Woods was at line-dancing class* again *last night...*

But I wasn't the only one doing sideways glances. While Dad was bent double, I caught Grandma and Stanley eyeing each other in the most peculiar way at the mere mention of the name "Daisy".

Why was that? What was the problem? Did it really upset Grandma to think of Dad liking someone else, someone who *wasn't* her daughter?

Good grief, paranoia strikes again...

Chapter 18

EMOTIONAL WIBBLE-WOBBLES

Can I just say that cake and cats don't mix?

OK, to be more accurate, wedding cake balanced on a spindly table and cats having a mad half-hour chasing each other round the living room don't mix.

"*Allleeeeee!*" Rowan called out in alarm from the top of the stepladder, where she was doing some last-minute streamer adjustments. "Catch it, *quick!*"

In a microsecond, I dropped the wispy bundle of cherubs I was holding and made a grab for the dangerously toppling table.

Phew! Got there just in time, before the cake went splat.

"I think we're going to have to lock the pets out of this room till we get back from the wedding," said Rowan, looking most peculiar in her new blue top and shell necklace, her hair a riot of crinkly crimpiness (thanks to sleeping with tiny plaits in), but still wearing her pyjama bottoms (her skirt was on the line, drying off in the morning sunshine after the work she'd done on it yesterday).

"Definitely," I agreed with her, checking that the layers of cake hadn't slid to one side, Leaning-Tower-of-Pisa-style, during my rescue mission just now. "We don't want all the guests to come back to a pile of crumbs and two fat, happy dogs snoozing underneath the... Uh-oh!"

"Uh-oh, what?" frowned Rowan, scampering down the stepladder to check out what had caught my attention.

"The cake decoration that Tor made – can you see what's wrong with it?" I grinned at her, pointing to the cute little blobby figurines that were supposed to be Grandma and Stanley.

"No. What is it?" said Rowan, scanning them for anything odd.

"Check out the little clay banner over their heads."

"Ah..."

There – *now* Ro got it. Tor had hand-painted the happy couple's names on the tiny, semi-circular banner.

"...'Grandma and Satanly'."

Yep. For a start, Tor hadn't really grasped the fact that Grandma's friends etc. probably called her "Irene" and not "Grandma". And poor, sweet, kind Stanley was not in any way related to Satan.

"Well, too late to do anything about it. We'll just

have to hope no one else notices!" I said, automatically crossing my fingers.

"Or that they have a sense of humour if they do!" Rowan giggled. "But, God – look at the time, Ally! We have to finish getting dressed, and you haven't even *started*!"

True. It was 10.25 a.m., and I might not have been in my jim-jams (like Rowan half was), but I couldn't exactly turn up to the registrar's in the grass-stained shorts and vest top I was currently wearing.

"And Linn said she'd phone from Grandma's at half-ten to check up on us!" said Rowan urgently, reminding me of Linn's stern words before she headed round to our gran's to help her out.

With the threat of Linn breathing down our necks from afar, we shooed Colin and two cats that weren't Colin out of our unnaturally tidy and prettily decorated living room and shut the door, before zooming off to get ourselves – and not just the house – ready for the wedding.

Rowan hurried through to the kitchen, presumably pootling out into the garden to check up on the dryness (or otherwise) of her skirt. I pattered up the stairs, marvelling at how our comfy but scruffy home had been transformed inside and out into a bit of a fairy palace – mostly thanks to the amazing efforts of Rowan, with a little help from the rest of us (including me and Tor doing snail patrols to Ally Pally three times yesterday). Inside the house, there were cascades of delicate paper doves and cherubs, alongside chains of pink card hearts that were sprinkled with silver glitter. Rowan had also bought loads of white paper tablecloths and put them over all the surfaces, but first edged them in glued-on silver and pink sequins. Outside in the snail-and-slug-free garden, she'd directed Dad as he strung up loads of white fairy lights, all ready to flick on and transform the place when the sun went down.

But that wasn't all that had kept Rowan busy – the whole day yesterday, in between doing her interior decorator bit, she'd been in a frenzy of sewing and dyeing (hippy tie-dyeing, to be precise). Instead of being plain white, her layered skirt was now covered in swirls of the palest shades of pink, blue, green, and lilac. Tor's plain cream cargo pants had got the same treatment, and Tor was so delighted with the look (*and* with his new blue T-shirt with the dolphin on the front) that he'd run next door to show them off to our neighbours Michael and Harry. And it wasn't just Rowan's skirt that had got the psychedelic pastel treatment, it was also—

"Dad?" I said with a start, hurrying along the attic landing towards my room and then stopping dead as I caught sight of him sitting silently at my desk.

It wasn't the fact that Dad was *in* there that had given me a shock – *or* the fact that he looked so unusually smart in his button-down white shirt and thin-lapelled grey suit. (It was an original 1960s Mod suit that he'd got married in, and that still fitted him.)

What *really* made me jump was what he was *looking* at.

Omigod, why hadn't I tidied those away...?

Last night, I'd been exhausted after a hard – and fun – day's decorating, but my brain was buzzing too much to let me sleep. Partly it was buzzing through sheer excitement, and partly it was buzzing with thoughts of Mum. And that's when I'd opened the drawer in my desk and dragged out all the journals I'd been keeping these last few months, packed full of the stories I'd written about me and my family and my friends and all scribbled there for Mum's benefit, so that when – *if* – she ever came home, she wouldn't feel like she'd missed out on anything.

In the end, I spent *ages* flicking through those journals, re-reading all the stuff I'd written about the time we lost Tor (eek!), about Rowan's shop-lifting episode (blee), about Linn and her disastrous boyfriend Q (git), about the time I went to school dressed as her (Mum), about Grandma meeting Stanley (awww), about Kyra and Sandie and Britney the pigeon and all the other people and pets Mum has never met (sadly). I re-read all the funny stuff and all the sad stuff and about all the times I thought of Mum and missed her, feeling close to her only when I was sticking pins in my map of the world, keeping track of every country she sent letters from.

Those journals had only been meant to be seen by me ... and Mum, hopefully, of course. But now here was Dad, his dark eyes scanning over the masses of words I'd set down.

"I didn't mean to be so nosey, Ally!" he said quickly, looking just as startled as me at being caught. "I came up to see how you were doing, and ... and I, well, spotted these lying open here. Once I saw what they were, I couldn't stop."

"That's OK," I shrugged, feeling bashful, even though I was talking to my own dad.

"You've been writing all these for Mum? All this time?" he asked, his brown eyes full of an expression I couldn't quite put my finger on. He seemed amazed, maybe even impressed, but somehow he also seemed, well, *emotionally* wibbly-wobbly too...

"I like doing it," I shrugged again, stepping over towards him and leaning one hand on the back of the chair he was sitting on. "It was fun. I only meant to write little bits, but every time I started they just turned out a trillion kilometres long, somehow."

It was funny – I thought I'd freak out if I ever found anyone reading this stuff, but I was glad now that Dad had come across it. I felt relieved, like I wasn't bottling up a secret any more, even though Dad knew most of what was in there. (Well, maybe not the stuff about Rowan and Linn having gone into pubs underage, but hopefully he wouldn't have spotted that from his quick flick...)

"It's tough sometimes, isn't it?" Dad murmured, reaching out and putting his arm around my waist. "Missing her, I mean?"

"Do you miss her lots, then?" I asked, pretty sure of what his answer would be.

"I miss her every day," he smiled up at me with sad eyes. "I miss hearing her laughing, and I miss her coming up with stupid colour schemes to paint the house, and I miss her coming in from the garden with handfuls of weeds to stick in a jar 'cause she thought they were as pretty as proper flowers and felt sorry for them 'cause no one else likes them."

I smiled at that, vaguely remembering the floppy bunches of weeds ("*Wild* flowers, Ally!") that Mum always used to place lovingly in an old, painted Nescafé jar in the middle of the kitchen table.

"And *most* of all," Dad continued, "I miss her when I look at any of you kids."

Us ... her Love children; that's what she calls us. *Called* us.

God, why was I suddenly thinking of her in the past tense, like she didn't exist any more? Maybe it was because – despite what he just said – I was terrified that Dad was starting to think of her that way.

"Dad..."

"What?" he asked, squeezing my waist as if that would squeeze out whatever question I wanted an answer to.

"Do you..." I gulped, wondering how to phrase this. "Do you think you could ever love someone as much as Mum? Someone like ... like Daisy Woods, I mean?"

"Wow!" he said in surprise. "*Daisy*? Well ... well, I do *like* Daisy..."

He seemed flummoxed, as if it had never

occurred to him that Daisy and him could be A Something.

"...but I've only met her a few times, Ally; she's just a friend."

Ah, but Dad – friends don't "twinkle" at each other like you and Daisy do... I thought to myself, wondering if *I* was more aware of what was going on with Daisy and Dad than Daisy and Dad were at the moment.

"And it's way, way, *way* too early to go thinking about us being anything more than friends," he tried to reassure me. "As for love, well, I don't think I could come close to loving *anyone* as much as I love your mum."

When he said that, it felt like my heart was made out of melted toffee and someone was gently *stretching* it and *twisting* it. It seemed like a good time for a hug, before Dad saw how watery my eyes were.

Great. Full-on sobs were just on the horizon, and that's all I'd need at the wedding; puffy, red eyes and nose to clash with my – blee! – pastel clothes. I'd have to pretend I'd just developed hayfever for the first time in my life...

"Daaaaddddd! Allleeeeeeee!! Come quickkkkkk!" we heard Rowan call up urgently from downstairs.

"What's up, Rowan?" Dad called back in

concern, as me and him discontinued our comfy, comforting hug.

"Winslet's stolen the streamers for the kitchen! She's running around the garden with them! And Rolf's trying to bury his squeaky toy in one of the planters of Grandma's begonias!!"

Well, Grandma's wedding or not, emotional wibble-wobbles or not, it was business as usual in the Love household...

Chapter 19

HUGE SURPRISE, NO. 3

"I'm going to hold Grandma's hand. *And* Stanley's," Tor announced, zooming away from me and my sisters.

We were standing in a little arc beside a table weighed down by a huge, but fake, flower arrangement. The registrar had positioned us there since we were bridesmaids. No one else was standing to attention like us; they were all – including Grandma and Stanley and Dad – mingling and chatting in the minute or two before the wedding officially began.

"Tor, come back! Stay here with us!" Rowan tried calling out after him, as he ran off.

"Oh, leave him alone," Linn told her, but not grumpily (for once). "Grandma won't mind."

I think the three of us were the only ones who were truly nervous – all the dressed-up friends and family were acting like they were at a party. Even Grandma seemed smiley and relaxed, holding her hand out to Tor and laughing at whatever he was now saying to her.

"So ... who's the woman with the chiffon spaceship on her head?" I hissed within hearing distance of my sisters, as I checked out some old lady in a scary hat in the gathering crowd of people here to celebrate Grandma and Stanley getting hitched.

"Think it's Stanley's sister," Linn hissed back.

"Grandma looks lovely, doesn't she?" Rowan whispered.

"Yes," me and Linn whispered back in reply.

She did. She was wearing a long, straight cream satin skirt with a matching jacket, and was carrying – as planned – a bouquet of pastel roses, that weren't at *all* blee. And speaking of looking nice, me and my sisters might not have looked remotely like ourselves, but I had to admit we were looking pretty nice too, and it was all thanks to Rowan. She'd pulled our mismatching marshmallow-coloured outfits together by making the most gorgeous, floppy, tie-dyed fabric roses, all in the same shades of pink, blue, lilac and soft green as her hippy skirt and Tor's trousers. Those roses were just *so* cool; the sort of thing you'd see in magazine fashion pages, or for sale in shops like Oasis or whatever, no kidding. Rowan had sewn one floppy rose on to a safety pin, and Linn was wearing it on the lapel of her lilac suit jacket. Rowan had sewn another one on to a hair slide, and had that clipped into her tangle of dark crimped hair. The last rose she sewed on to a length of dusky pink velvet, and I was now wearing that around my neck, while my shell necklace from Mum was wrapped around my wrist, doubling up as a bracelet.

And Rowan hadn't just stopped there. The dilemma we all had about what shoes to wear with pastel clothes? Rowan had sorted that by rummaging amongst the magazine racks in four separate newsagents on Thursday evening till she'd got what she wanted. It seemed that several different magazines had flip-flops as special free gifts for summer. Rowan finally found the perfect match, and now we were wearing them: pink flip-flops with a pink, plastic rosebud on each one for me; lilac flip-flops with a purply starfish on each one for Linn; and blue flip-flops with a blue daisy-thing on each one for Rowan. Yep, amazingly, we all kind of *went* together. I tell you, it was nothing short of a miracle. She may be an airhead, but Rowan should get a job as a stylist for magazines or pop videos or something for *sure*.

"Ooh, look!" I muttered, spotting a cute-looking guy wearing a badly fitting black suit, heavy metal T-shirt and dreadlocks. "That must be Stanley's rebel grandson Jamie!"

"Cute!" gushed Rowan, while I noticed Linn wrinkling her nose.

But we didn't get much time to gawp at Jamie, *or* the woman in the spaceship hat, *or* anyone else. The registrar was bustling back in, taking his place behind the table next to us and motioning for the guests to take their seats, while gesturing to Grandma and Stanley to come forward.

Make that, Grandma and Stanley and *Tor*.

Dad had to step forward and extricate Tor from in between them both, so they had a chance to hold each other's hands (aww!), instead of his.

"Are we ready to begin?" the registrar beamed.

I spotted Grandma glance down quickly at her watch, then give Stanley a funny look.

"Yes, we are," Stanley said loudly, smiling such a huge, warm smile at Grandma that she burst into a smile herself.

"Lovely," the registrar pronounced brightly. "Well, it gives me *great* pleasure to announce, as you all know, that we are gathered here today to witness the happy union of Irene and Stanley. So with no further ado, let's…"

I went into a kind of contented trance as I listened to the registrar begin trotting out words that I'd heard loads of times before, in films and on TV, when various characters did the wedding thing.

But this is real! I tried to tell myself as I gazed in awe at my gran and Stanley, and reminded myself to *breathe*.

Plenty of others amongst the guests were remembering to breathe out as the ceremony went on – I was aware of happy sighs, blown noses, kids gabbling, parents and grandparents shushing, chairs squeaking, even the door to the room thunking gently as some last-minute guest slunk in from the bathroom or wherever they'd been.

But even though I was vaguely aware of all that, I couldn't drag my eyes away from the amazing sight of my gran and Stanley gazing at each other, as if they were sixteen and in love instead of sixty-something and in love, as they said "I do".

I knew it must be getting close to the end – the bit when the registrar would say, "I pronounce you ... etc., etc.", but I was suddenly distracted by a movement from the corner of my eye – it was Tor, holding hands with Dad, but twisting around in his seat, staring at the back of the room. I thought nothing of it, and looked back at Grandma and Stanley.

"...man and wife. You may kiss the bride!" the registrar boomed happily."

And as Stanley did what he was told and kissed Grandma, everyone began cheering and clapping.

Everyone except Tor ... who was still staring – staring *hard* – towards the back of the room. I glanced round, trying to see what he could see, and then...

And then I saw.

I saw.

I saw her.

I saw *her*.

"Mum...?" I heard myself muttering under my breath.

Only it wasn't a mutter under my breath. It was more of a loud squeak (Linn told me later).

And with that, *everyone* turned to see the woman with the long, tumbling, sun-bleached hair, holding hands with a tiny dark-haired girl in a pink dress and cute, matching, pink sunhat...

Chapter 20

HUGE (SMALL) SURPRISE, NO. 4

I had a mum.

I mean, I'd *always* had a mum, but not one in the same room as me, not for a long time. Not one that I'd been able to hug, or that could hug me back. And there she was now, sitting on the sofa in a floaty sea-green dress, looking like a beautiful, nervously smiling, lightly tanned mirage.

And there was Something Else. It was only a small Something Else, but it was a mind-blowingly, mega-important Something Else. You want to know? Well it seems I had a sister.

I mean, *we* had a sister. I mean... I mean that I *don't* mean Linn and Rowan.

(Could you tell my head was mince?)

I *mean*, me, Linn, Rowan and Tor ... we all had a sister we never knew about. Dad had a daughter he never knew about. Grandma had a grand-daughter she ... well, Grandma *did* know about her but more of that in a minute.

"How old are you?" Tor asked the little girl with

the brown bob who was sitting on the sofa, her feet in her little pink sandals dangling way above the floor.

He was crouched down by the side of the sofa, staring up at her. It had taken a while for Tor to work his way over there (the whole time Mum had been talking and explaining everything to us). In fact, when we arrived back here after the wedding, Tor had started out perched on Linn's lap, staring from a safe distance at Mum and...

"Ivy?" Mum smiled at our sister in that dreamily familiar way of hers. "Tell Tor how old you are!"

Instead of talking, the little girl in the pink sunhat (and pink everything), raised up four fingers on her hand, then bent one of them over.

"She's three and a half!" Tor announced excitedly to me, Linn, Tor, Dad and Grandma.

Wow. Had Tor met his match? Was there a Love child who spoke less than him?

Mind you, the rest of us Love children had been pretty quiet too, for the last half-hour. I'd always imagined that when – *if* – Mum turned up again, we'd all run towards her together, like one giant, smiling, crying, human bundle of happiness. Well, we'd done that all right, but now it was as if we all felt *shy* or something. Rowan might have been superglued to her side, staring at Mum as if she was scared she'd vanish again, but me and Linn – like Dad – seemed rooted to our seats. I guess sitting here together in the streamer-decked living room, while all the wedding guests were partying (in a subdued way, I guess) in the rest of the house and garden made the whole situation totally surreal for us all.

"Why are you called Ivy?" Tor asked the serious little girl in the sunhat.

I couldn't quite take in that she was my sister yet.

"She's called Ivy, after St Ives, Tor," Mum smiled down at him. Her hand trembled, as if she wanted to reach out and touch him, stroke his spiky, dark hair, but didn't dare to.

"St Ives in Cornwall. Where Mum's been living," Grandma explained to him.

Where Grandma had secretly gone to visit Mum a few months ago, in an effort to persuade her to come home. It turned out that Mum had contacted Grandma way back last year, but had felt too nervous to get in touch with Dad and us after being gone so long. Poor Grandma had spent all this time trying to convince her to come home, but never breathed a word of it to us because she'd sworn to keep Mum's secret. Mum's *secrets*, as it turned out, since Ivy wasn't the only one. The other was that Mum had never left the country in all the time she'd been gone! You want the whole, bizarre, mad, insane, bonkers, brain-cell-melting story? Well, it went like this...

Three years after Tor was born, Mum, suffering from some kind of freaky, long-drawn-out baby blues (post-natal depression, as it's properly called) decided to pack a rucksack and go travelling on her own for a few weeks, starting with a quick visit to her old school pal who now lived in St Ives, Cornwall. This much we all knew.

What we *didn't* know was that she'd never – in the past few years – travelled any further than St Ives. While she was staying with her friend, the old familiar morning sickness had started and Mum realized that she was going to have a baby. She – and Dad, of course – hadn't realized she was pregnant before she'd even set off.

But because Mum wasn't thinking straight at the time, she didn't do the obvious thing and come back home. She'd been desperate to see the world, and couldn't bear to give up her dream, so – thanks to her strange, not-very-well way of thinking – she buried her head in the sand (and there's a lot of it about at the beach in St Ives) and stayed where she was.

For months, she worked in her friend's craft

shop, painting pictures and T-shirts and making and selling her funny sculptures, becoming matey with all the passing tourists from all over the world who dropped by. After a while she had Ivy, but as much as her friend tried to persuade her to get in touch with Dad and us all, Mum wouldn't. Her thinking was still muddled, and she thought we'd all be mad at her for only being five hours by train away from us and never telling us about Ivy. And the longer she stayed away, the more sure she was that we'd all forget her or resent her or both.

In the meantime, she went back to work at the craft shop, and carried on with the weird habit she'd started up – taking pictures of herself in different poses on St Ives beach (waving, paddling, eating ice-cream), writing letters, giving them to tourists she'd made friends with and asking them to post them to us from wherever their homelands were; from Canada to the Cook Islands, from Thailand to Tahiti to Texas…

Oh, yes.

Silent as I was, suddenly a million things slotted into place as Mum poured out her story.

"It never made sense," I heard myself croak out loud.

"What didn't, Ally?" Mum asked me, bringing me out in goosebumps as her green eyes gazed at me.

"When I stuck the pins on the map to show where your letters were from. Sometimes, it was like you travelled halfway around the world then back again in only a few days."

Mum bit her lip and pulled an apologetic face, but didn't try to make excuses for herself.

"And sometimes," Rowan piped up, now that I'd started the ball rolling, "you'd write about stuff like being at the beach, but your letters were stamped from cities or countries that weren't anywhere *near* the sea."

Mum nodded sadly, caught out again. (Ivy was now being sniffed by a curious cat that wasn't Colin. She started sniffing him back, oblivious to how uncomfortable Mum looked beside her.)

"And two photos you sent last month?" I carried on, as more examples flooded into my head. "One was supposed to be from Dallas and one from Hawaii – but both of them had the same Golden Retriever bounding about behind you!"

"Ben!" squeaked Ivy, uttering the first word we'd heard her utter.

"Our dog," shrugged Mum in explanation.

"Yeah?" Tor's face lit up.

"You know, we thought you were psychic," Linn jumped in, before Tor could ask any dog-related questions. "When you sent us stuff like that new fairy for the top of the tree last Christmas, and the shell necklaces for Grandma's wedding ... they were perfect. We thought you somehow just *guessed* what we needed or wanted. But it was Grandma telling you, wasn't it?"

Mum scrunched her eyes closed, as if she couldn't bear the guilt as we all stared questioningly at her.

"And those weird phone calls to do with the wedding!" I burst out, turning to Grandma. "That was you talking to Mum, wasn't it?"

In particular, I remembered Stanley explaining to me that Grandma was trying to persuade an "old friend" to come to the wedding. He was stuffing travel tickets in an envelope at the time – probably train tickets for Mum and Ivy...

"Yes, she *was* talking to me," Mum said, answering me instead of Grandma, opening her eyes and giving me a smile that was halfway between being wry and apologetic. "I kept changing my mind about coming. I got it in my head that I'd spoil your gran's wedding day if I turned up out of the blue in front of everyone..."

Grandma rolled her eyes, but smiled at the same time.

"Your mother took a lot of persuading, let me tell you," she stated. "Mostly I called her from my own flat at night, but there was so much to-ing and fro-ing going on that a couple of times I was forced to phone her from here, when you children were out."

"Only we kept spoiling it by walking in on you, didn't we, Grandma?" I pointed out.

"Yes," Grandma nodded and laughed softly. "I'm not very good at all this cloak and dagger stuff. You nearly gave me an ulcer with it all, Melanie!"

"Sorry, Mum!" said *our* mum, wrinkling her nose and wincing in Grandma's direction. "I just didn't want to mess up your wedding, considering I've managed to mess everything else up for the last four years…"

Everyone went quiet as Mum's voice trailed off. I noticed that Dad looked like he was on the verge of moving towards her, and then seemed to stop himself, and sat stiffly where he was, his face clouded in confusion.

"You didn't mess things up, Mum!" Rowan broke the silence and assured her, squeezing her arm tight. "Seeing you at the wedding today was the best thing ever!"

"Last night, when your gran and Stanley came round to the hotel me and Ivy are staying in, I told them that I'd *definitely* decided not to come – that it just wasn't fair on them, on all of you," Mum explained.

"And *I* told *you* to sleep on it," Grandma replied. "I didn't give up hope that you'd change your mind, Melanie, and I'm so glad you did."

Mum gave Grandma a shy little smile that was instantly familiar – in that second, she looked *exactly* like a blondish version of Rowan. How weird...

"But weren't you even going to tell us that Mum was here, in Crouch End?" Linn jumped in. "I mean, if she hadn't turned up at the wedding, she might have gone away again without us knowing she was so close!"

"I was hoping your mum might still come round here afterwards, even if she didn't want to come to the wedding itself."

"But what if she *hadn't*, Grandma!" Linn demanded of Grandma, as if Mum wasn't even there. And before Mum got a chance to explain herself some more, someone else spoke.

"Linn, I think your gran was just trying to do the right thing and let your mum decide what to do in her own time," said a pale-faced Dad, breaking his silence at last. "Isn't that right, Melanie?"

"But—" Linn started up again, before she was interrupted.

"OK, I think that's enough questions for now," Grandma announced, standing up. "I think we should all leave and give your mum and dad a little time on their own, don't you? Ally – do you want to take Ivy and Tor out to the garden?"

In a haze, I did what I was told, ushering my little brother and little sister (!), out in front of me to the sun-dappled, guest-filled garden.

"Hi, Ally! What's going on? Where have you all been?"

Sandie's smiling face was suddenly hovering in front of me, along with Kyra's, and Billy's too. But from their body language (i.e. Billy was standing *miles* away from Sandie) it didn't seem like the two of them would be doing much smiling at each other.

"Yeah, what's the big deal? Everyone around here seems to be doing a lot of whispering!" said Kyra, staring round at the groups of chatting guests. Those people who'd been at the wedding knew what had happened – but did nearly everyone else too?

I couldn't help noticing Daisy, standing with some of Dad's friends from line-dancing class. She was listening to someone talking. Her mouth was smiling – but her eyes were sad and full of disappointment. *She* knew. You know, I was so deliriously happy (and just plain *delirious*) to have

Mum back, but right that second I couldn't help feeling really, really sorry for Miss Woods...

"Hey, who's the kid?" Billy asked in his usual blunt way, staring down at Ivy, who was standing in front of me, pushing up the rim of her pink sunhat and staring straight back up at him.

"She's ... she's Ivy," I began to explain. "She's my sister. Mum's back!"

Sandie opened her mouth so wide you could have fitted a doughnut in it, no problem. Kyra too was shocked into total silence, which – if you know anything about Kyra – is a very rare occurrence. Only Billy spoke. Or make that *squeaked*.

"God, yeah! Look at them! They're *identical*!" he said, pointing at an earnest Tor and an equally earnest Ivy. "Matching spook-kids! Cool!"

Even if Kyra and Sandie had managed to find their voices, there wasn't time to tell them any more – Stanley was clanging a spoon on a glass and calling for everyone's attention. I turned around, spying Linn and Rowan hurriedly shooing Rolf away, *just* as he was about to lift his leg against the trestle table Grandma and Stanley were now standing beside, as they got ready to cut their cake.

"I'd like to say a quick word!" Stanley called out, his voice sounding a little nervous or emotional or something. "I'm not very good at speeches. So all I'd like to say is –"

He turned to Grandma, his face all smiles.

"– I'm absolutely over the moon to be married to such a wonderful woman. And although I'm very lucky to have my own family, I'm delighted that I've inherited Irene's wonderful family too – even though it seems to get bigger by the minute!"

There was a ripple of laughter from all the guests crowded in the garden, and then a cheer as Stanley raised his glass of champagne to Grandma.

Behind him in the kitchen doorway, I spotted Mum and Dad, lifting up the glasses they were holding and clinking them together, with funny, shy little smiles on their faces.

Gulp.

Just as a prickle of a tear started threatening in my left eye, I felt a small, warm hand slide into mine.

"Are you OK, Ivy?" I smiled down at the serious little girl with Tor's Malteser-brown eyes.

Her face broke into a smile, showing off her dainty baby teeth.

Wow, I thought, *this might just be the most wonderfully weird and weirdly wonderful day of my life...*

Chapter 21

EXTRA, ADDED HAPPINESS

"So," said Billy, holding Sandie's hand tight. "Sandie's not the *only* one to have a baby sister, then!"

"I guess not," I'd laughed at the party last night, marvelling at the marvellousness of everything, including Billy and Sandie getting back together.

Yesterday's party had blurred by in a haze of happiness for me. I know you're *meant* to be happy at weddings, but with the surprise of Mum and Ivy turning up, it felt like everyone at the reception was *extra* happy. Billy and Sandie couldn't *help* but be infected by all that added happiness in the atmosphere, and were smooching and making up before Kyra and me knew it.

And then there was the dancing. *Everyone* was dancing. Hours and hours of giggling and swirling to all sorts of music under the glitter and gleam of the fairy lights. I danced with Kyra and Billy and Sandie, I danced with Stanley, I danced with Michael and then Harry from next door. I danced with Stanley's elderly sister Maisie and his rebel grandson Jamie. I danced with Linn and Alfie (sigh!), I danced with Rowan (her mates Von and Chazza were the only people who were too "cool" to dance). I danced with Daisy Woods (who was lovely and told me she was *so* happy for us that Mum was back). And I danced with Tor and Ivy and Rolf, till Tor got bored and dragged Ivy away to go on snail patrol (she loved it – I spotted her later, stroking a slug).

And this morning, I still felt great, even though I knew not *everything* was quite perfect. Mum was back sleeping in her old bedroom all right, but with Ivy keeping her company, and not Dad (who'd slept on the spare blow-up bed in Tor's room).

I was just staring at the map on my wall, wondering if I should take it down now that I didn't have to worry where Mum was (downstairs at the kitchen table, last time I looked), when I heard a tapping at my bedroom door.

"Can I come in?" asked Mum hesitantly, her fair hair tumbling over her shoulders.

"Of course!" I grinned at her, studying every distantly familiar move as she padded barefoot into my room.

"I found this in the wardrobe – I'd forgotten all about it!" she explained, holding out the loose, blue hippy sundress that she must have thought I was staring at. "And I'd forgotten how *amazing* this view is!"

I followed her over and joined her as she gazed out of the window at the sight of Alexandra Palace sitting perched on its hill.

"We could go there today!" I told her excitedly. "I take the dogs for walks up Ally Pally all the time!"

Mum smiled at me, slipping her arm around my shoulders and giving me a squeeze. She looked like she wanted to say something but didn't know how to start.

"I ... I just wanted to have a chat with you all. On your own," she began.

I held my breath, hoping that what she was about to say wasn't going to make all this extra, added happiness slip away...

"It's just that ... things can't just slot back exactly as they were, Ally. I've been away for too long, and too many things have gone on for that to happen. Do you understand?"

I nodded, still giddy through lack of oxygen.

"Does that mean you're going away again?" I asked, feeling my heart go *crunch* at the thought of her – and Ivy – disappearing on us as quickly as they appeared.

"I've got to be honest with you; I don't know

what that means long-term, Ally. But me and Ivy, we're going to stick around for a week or two, if that's all right. Just to give me and Dad a chance to do some talking. Would that be OK with you?"

Would that be OK with me? Was she *kidding*?

"After that, well, we'll just have to wait and—"

A thundering and squealing from the stairwell stopped Mum's sentence in mid-air. We both turned round to see Ivy (in pink PJs and clutching Mad Max the hamster) and Tor (in Spiderman jim-jams and toast crumbs round his mouth) come screeching and giggling into my bedroom, with Dad chasing them – roaring and growling – on all fours, followed by a panting Rolf and Winslet.

You know, you've never seen two kids, a grown man, two daft dogs and a bad-tempered hamster look so happy.

Or me…

Love you lots, Mum (and now I KNOW you're really reading this),

Ally :c) & xxxxxxxxxxxxx times a trillion

PS Billy and Sandie are nearly back to being my ace best friends, even though they're totally lovey-dovey again. Today, Billy even came over all sensitive, cycling round with an article he'd seen in his parents' Sunday magazine about why people run away from home. It was actually about teenagers (and not thirty-something-year-old mums), but it was really sweet of him. The big soppy berk.

PPS Remember Tor's misspelt banner on the wedding cake figurines? Well, plenty of eagle-eyed guests spotted that, including Stanley's sister, Maisie, who spent quite a while frowning at it. Unlike Stanley, who thought it was so excellent that he insisted they keep the figurines as a memento, and now the mini "Grandma and Satanly" have pride of place on their mantlepiece.

PPPS Tor and Ivy are inseparable. She talks less than him, but that's fine with Tor. She is crazy about animals and was thrilled when Britney landed on her head in the garden. Tor likes Ivy so much that he gave her his favourite toy, Mr Penguin. And he hasn't mentioned "Troy" for days. But who needs an imaginary friend when you have a real-life instant sister?

PPPPS Spotted Dad putting his arm round Mum's waist in the garden last night when they didn't think anyone was looking. I'm keeping my fingers crossed so tight that I think I might be stopping the circulation in them... Blee!

SIGN UP NOW!

For exclusive news, competitions and further information about Karen and her books, sign up to the Karen McCombie newsletter now!

Just email

publicity@scholastic.co.uk

And don't forget to check out her website –

www.karenmccombie.com

brain full of plots, stupid stuff and cat hair

KM^cC

the author

Karen says…

"It's sheeny and shiny, furry and er, funny in places! It's everything you could want from a website and a weeny bit more…"

KaReN McCombie

"A funny and talented author"
Books Magazine

Once upon a time (OK, 1990), Karen McCombie jumped in her beat-up car with her boyfriend and a very bad-tempered cat, leaving her native Scotland behind for the bright lights of London and a desk at "J17" magazine. She's lived in London and acted like a teenager ever since.

The fiction bug bit after writing short stories for "Sugar" magazine. Next came a flurry of teen novels, and of course the best-selling "Ally's World" series, set around and named after Alexandra Palace in North London, close to where Karen lives with her husband Tom, little daughter Milly and an assortment of cats.

Funny FAQs

When I do talks at schools, book shops, libraries and festivals, I get asked lots of interesting, sensible questions about me, my life, and writing my books. And then I get the NSFAQs (Not So Frequently Asked Questions). Check out some below!

Do you live in a mansion?

Er, nope. Until a couple of years ago, we lived in a very nice two-bedroomed flat - then we moved round the corner to a three-bedroomed terraced house, which we added a loft room office to. We've got a swimming pool, though. (OK, it's a metre-wide blow-up paddling pool, decorated with freaky-looking dolphins that our daughter Milly loves!)

Are you Scottish?

Well, I have a very Scottish last name and a Scottish accent, so, I guess, yes - I AM pretty Scottish! But I've lived in London since 1990, so I consider myself very much Britishish).

What's your favourite football team?

Er, don't have one. If there's such a thing at football dyslexia, I think I may have it. When I try and watch a match on TV, all I see is a jumble of legs running and can't figure out who's who, or where they're headed.

What's your favourite colour?

Yellow to look at, green to wear. But I'm pretty addicted to looking at colours: from the pink of cherry blossoms to the peach of sunsets to the weird rainbow swirls of oil in a puddle...

To: You
From: Stella
Subject: Stuff

Hi,

You'd think it would be cool to live by the sea with all that sun, sand and ice cream. But, believe me, it's not such a breeze. I miss my best mate Frankie, my terror twin brothers drive me nuts and my mum and dad have gone daft over the country dump, sorry, "character cottage", that we're living in. I'm bored, and I'm fed up with being the new girl on the block.
Hey! Maybe if we hang out together we could have some fun here. Whadya think?
Catch up with me in the rest of the *Stella Etc.* series.
I bet we'll have loads to talk about.
CU soon.
LOL

stella
XXX

PS Here's a pic of me on a bad hair day (any day actually) with my mate Frankie. I'm the one on the right!

"Super-sweet and cool as an ice cream" *Mizz*

ALLY'S WORLD

Hi,
There's lots going on in my world – here's just some of what I have to deal with!!

3 SISTERS – 1 bOSSY,
1 bONKERS, 1 PiNK
1 SPACE-CAdet bROtheR
1 dad
0 MUM
1 SCRUffY hoUSE iN a NiCE PLACE
with a fUNNY NAME
1 gReat View fROM MY bedROOM
2 dOgS – WiNSLet aNd ROLf
(dON't eVeN aSk)
5 cats – 1'S CaLLEd COLiN
Oh, aNd fRiENdS – LOts.

Now that you've finished this story, get into one of my other adventures – there's heaps to choose from.

"Once you start reading you can't stop" *Mizz*